BATGIRL™
at SUPER HERO HIGH

By Lisa Yee

Random House 🏠 New York

To my best friend Henry, who is super smart

All rights reserved. Published in the United States by Random House Children's
Books, a division of Penguin Random House LLC, 1745 Broadway, New York, NY
10019, and in Canada by Penguin Random House Canada Limited, Toronto. Random
House and the colophon are registered trademarks of Penguin Random House LLC.
randomhousekids.com
dcsuperherogirls.com
ISBN 978-1-101-94065-5 (hc) — ISBN 978-1-101-94066-2 (lib. bdg.)
ISBN 978-1-101-94067-9 (ebook)
Printed in the United States of America
10 9 8 7 6 5 4 3 2 1

PROLOGUE

Oh, sure, there were injuries. Lumps and bruises were an occupational hazard. Sometimes it was because a muscle-bound metahuman was momentarily careless when working out in Wildcat's phys ed class. Or because a flyer took a turn a tad too sharply and slammed into a wall (or a fellow student or the cafeteria) at full speed. Or because of something like what had just happened: an invading interstellar alien army had targeted the student population for total enslavement to the powers of evil . . . which was all part of the daily routine at Super Hero High School. And most of the super heroes in training loved it.

Now, as the young heroes flew, ran, stretched, strolled, and teleported into the auditorium, they laughed and congratulated each other. They admired their new casts and bandages and bruises. Never had so many been so sore—and so happy about it.

"Not everyone likes a bump on the noggin, but everyone likes the attention," the class clown Harley Quinn said merrily as she uploaded an exclusive video to Harley's Quinntessentials, her "All Harley, All the Time" video channel. The footage showed fashionista Star Sapphire sneaking on a couture neck brace she didn't need.

A loud cough reverberated from the stage.

All heads snapped to the front and faced the imposing figure.

"Super Heroes, you have much to be proud of!" boomed Principal Amanda "The Wall" Waller. Her elite students had battled malevolent Granny Goodness and her army of Furies, thwarting the villains' plan to take over the world. Best of all, no lives had been lost. And at Super Hero High, the goal was to save the world and cause as little damage as possible while doing so.

In back of the auditorium, Parasite, the janitor, swept with his left arm. The cast on his right arm matched his blue-gray uniform and complemented his purple face. He nodded cheerfully before remembering to be grumpy. Cleaning up the messes super hero teens made was not his idea of fun. (And there were *always* messes.)

Waller suppressed a smile. She was not one of those "let's be friends!" feel-good principals. Still, she said, "Students, teachers, staff, give yourselves a well-deserved round of applause!"

After allowing the cheering to go on for several rowdy minutes, The Wall arched an eyebrow and the room went silent. Everyone leaned forward and soaked up the praise she heaped on them. Amanda Waller was known more for her sharp constructive criticism than for her compliments, so the Supers savored this moment, smiling at one another.

"And now," Principal Waller continued, "it's time to announce our Super Hero of the Month."

No one dared move, and Miss Martian couldn't because Killer Frost had just frozen her, "as a joke." The only sound in the cavernous auditorium was a tiny *ping* coming from Cyborg's internal circuitry.

"Supergirl!" Waller called out.

The auditorium erupted in cheers for its newest student. She had proven herself under the most serious of circumstances and had put her own life at risk to save others.

As Supergirl sat stunned, Bumblebee flew over and nudged her friend toward the stage. "M-m-me?" Supergirl stammered, still in shock. She pushed her blond bangs out of her eyes. "Me?"

"Yes, you!" Bumblebee said gleefully. Katana bowed to Supergirl, and Beast Boy cheered. Supergirl tried not to trip—she did that a lot—as she made her way up the aisle.

Asked to say a few words, Supergirl choked back her tears. *How is it possible to be both happy and sad at the same time?* the young alien wondered. Supergirl wished her parents were there to see her, but that was impossible. She hoped Harley was videoing so she could share this moment with Aunt Martha and Uncle Jonathan. As she stood on the stage thanking everyone for their teamwork, some noticed that Supergirl also kept looking up and would pause to speak into a slim bracelet that graced her wrist.

"I couldn't have done it without you," Supergirl whispered into it. "You helped me become who I am. You helped save the world from Granny Goodness and her army. You deserve to be up here, too."

In the rafters, looking down at the assembly, a girl dressed in black replied wistfully, "In my dreams, Supergirl. In my dreams."

Supergirl covered the microphone and spoke to the principal. Both looked serious. Liberty Belle, Doc Magnus, and Police Commissioner Gordon, all teachers who were sitting on the stage, glanced at one another. The Supers shifted in their seats. Finally, Waller nodded and stepped away as Supergirl spoke into the microphone. . . .

"There is someone in this room who was invaluable in fighting the epic battle. Without this person, multiple lives would have been lost," she began. "I would like to publicly acknowledge their epic contribution."

Many of the Supers, like Katana, Frost, and Adam Strange, sat tall, each convinced she was talking about them. Hal Jordan, the first earthling to be made a member of the intergalactic peacekeeping force known as the Green Lantern Corps, was especially sure it must be him. He wasn't bigheaded about it, but he was proud to be called a Green Lantern.

"Batgirl," Supergirl called. "Please join us!"

PART ONE

CHAPTER 1

Nothing happened.

Supergirl stood alone.

A low murmur swept the auditorium. Had the battle caused her to lose it? Supers all reacted to combat differently. Some were energized, others needed time alone, and a few never wanted to fight again.

Supergirl didn't move.

Instead, she kept looking up. Soon everyone else did, too, unsure of what or who they were looking for.

Finally, a mysterious figure swung gracefully from the rafters on a thin wire and landed silently on the stage. For a moment, no one said a word. Then everyone began talking at once, trying to figure out who the costumed figure was. She wasn't one of them. Who was behind the black mask? *Batgirl?* No one had ever heard of her.

It was Katana who spoke loudest. "Great costume!" she shouted. (She had, after all, helped design the elegantly functional black suit.) Then Katana whispered to Wonder Woman, who told Hawkgirl, who told Bumblebee Batgirl's true identity. Soon the entire student body was buzzing with the news.

"Everyone," Supergirl said, turning to the audience, "I want you to meet Batgirl! If it weren't for her, the battle against the Furies would have had a very different outcome. I couldn't have done all that I did without her help. She is one of us. She has the heart of a super hero!"

After the cheers died down and the shouts of "Yay for Batgirl!" and "Hooray for Supergirl!" trailed off, Waller gave her a nod and said, "Thank you, Batgirl. Super Hero High is in your debt." And with that, she added, "All right, people. We all played a part in saving the world, but now we have more work to do. Parasite can't get this place back into shape by himself."

The teachers and the Supers shuffled out of the auditorium. After all the excitement, no one was in a hurry to get back to class. But Waller was right. Parts of the school had been destroyed during the battle. There was work to be done. That didn't stop the students from whispering and theorizing about the mysterious new hero . . . who happened to be a familiar face around campus.

One teacher remained rooted to his chair, looking like he had seen a ghost. When he started coughing, Supergirl ran over to him and patted him on the back. But she had forgotten how strong she was and knocked him to the ground.

"So sorry, Commissioner Gordon," Supergirl said, looking down at her red high-top sneakers in embarrassment.

He got up wordlessly, but instead of looking at Supergirl, he stared at the girl dressed in black.

"*Bat*girl?" he asked. His jaw locked and his face was stern.

"Oh, hello, Commissioner Gordon, sir," Batgirl said nervously, lowering her voice in an effort to disguise it. "Um, nice to . . . er, nice to meet you, sir. Commissioner. Mister. Mr. Gordon. Sir. Mr. Commissioner Gordon, sir."

When she reached out to shake his hand, he did not take it. Instead, he said, "Barbara, we need to talk. You think I don't recognize my own daughter?"

Batgirl didn't answer. In a rare moment of uncertainty, she wasn't completely sure who she was.

"Barbara!" Commissioner Gordon barked. Even his mustache looked serious. "When I agreed to let you get a part-time job as the tech wizard for Super Hero High, that did not include you going into battle, or wearing a ridiculous costume, or pretending to be a super hero! Now get back into your own clothes and let's get you to Gotham City High School, where you belong."

"It's not a ridiculous costume!" Katana shouted from the back of the room. "It's sleek, stylish, and awesome."

"Come on, Katana," Poison Ivy said, ushering her friend out the door. "Let's see what shape the greenhouse is in after the Furies' attack."

"Batgirl's outfit is *not* ridiculous," Katana muttered,

gripping her sword. She was known as much for her artistically stylish creations as for wielding a sword with the strength, substance, and determination of twenty samurai warriors.

"Your daughter?" Doc Magnus, the new Robotics and Computer Science teacher, asked Commissioner Gordon on his way out. "You should be very proud of her achievement."

Commissioner Gordon gritted his teeth and forced a smile. "Yes, Barbara is an amazing tech expert."

"Well, yes, that. But for helping save lives," Doc Magnus added appreciatively. "Good job, Batgirl!"

"Her name is *Barbara*," Police Commissioner Gordon grumbled. Doc Magnus got the hint and walked away.

Barbara recognized her father's tone as the one he used when he had to listen to Mr. Morris complain about the "young whippersnappers" making too much noise outside his shoe repair store.

Her dad waited until almost everyone was gone. "What do you have to say for yourself?" he asked.

Barbara stood still, her posture ramrod straight, her demeanor unfazed. She swept her auburn hair over her shoulders and adopted a confident expression. Inside, though, her stomach was turning the kind of somersaults that even Harley Quinn would have been proud of.

"She's amazing," Supergirl chimed in. Barbara had almost forgotten that her best friend was still there. "She saved my life! Batgirl—er, Barbara is incredibly brave and smart, and *wow,* can she stay cool under pressure!"

Principal Waller stepped out from behind the heavy red velvet stage curtain. "Commissioner Gordon, Barbara knows more about high tech than anyone I have ever met, but she has a whole lot more to offer," The Wall began. "She has brains, bravery, and ingenuity. She is super hero material. Your daughter—"

Barbara cut in. "Excuse me, I don't mean to interrupt you," she said. "But may I have a moment alone with Commissioner Gordon?"

Waller turned to the Hero of the Month. "Supergirl," she said, "this does not concern us. This is between father and daughter."

Supergirl nodded. She wished she had a father she could talk to, even if he wanted to lecture her. When Supergirl touched her crystal necklace, it glowed with a soft white light.

Before leaving, Principal Waller said, "Police Commissioner Gordon, you know that Super Hero High is one of the few schools that recruit students based not on who they are today, but on who they could become tomorrow." He didn't blink. "I think . . . Wait. I *know* that Barbara has what it takes to be an incredible super hero, with the proper training. I would like to extend an open invitation to her to attend Super Hero High—with parental permission, of course."

Barbara's heart began to race. All her life she had wanted nothing more than to fight crime like her father. Her dream was to join the police force someday. It had never occurred to her that she could actually make a bigger difference as a super hero. And when she got the job handling the tech for Super Hero High, Barbara Gordon stood in the back of classrooms as she fixed computers and phones, recharged weapons, and rebooted Cyborg, her friend who was half man, half machine, all good-hearted. And all that time Barbara was also soaking in Super Hero History with Liberty Belle, admiring the costumes from Crazy Quilt's assignments, and marveling at Lucius Fox's Weaponomics class. To be a part of all this as a participant—an actual student—suddenly made Batgirl feel like her heart would burst with happiness. Not only would she be going to school with her best friend, Supergirl, but now she could honestly and truly test her skills. After all, the students at Super Hero High were the best of the best, and Barbara Gordon finally had a chance to prove that she was, too.

"No, just no," he was saying.

"What? But, Dad—"

"Barbara," her father said. His square shoulders slumped. "You are my only daughter. As your father, I am here to protect you, not throw you in harm's way. Besides, you're good at math. Maybe you could become an accountant, or work in a bank, or do something else. Something safe . . ."

Barbara blinked back her frustration. She could feel her

jaw tighten. Hadn't Waller just told him how perfect she would be as a student at Super Hero High? Here was a new dream being handed to her, and her father was tossing it all away.

"Dad," she began slowly. He had always taught her that when criminals lose their tempers, they lose their advantage. Not that either of them was a criminal—quite the contrary. "Give me one good reason why I shouldn't attend Super Hero High."

She waited, confident that she could refute whatever argument he had. As captain of the Gotham High debate team, Barbara Gordon was a great teammate and a feared but respected adversary.

"Because," her father replied, "I love you and don't ever want to see you get hurt." She began to speak but stopped herself when her father's eyes misted over and he added, "Because I couldn't live without you."

For once, Barbara Gordon didn't know what to say.

CHAPTER 2

Barbara had always been a great debater. Even as a toddler, she used wits and logic to get what she wanted. That last snickerdoodle? "It'll go stale if no one eats it." More school supplies? "The better to study with." A new computer? "By my calculations, the ability to shop online will save us money in the long run."

But how did one argue with someone else's feelings? That stumped her.

After school, Barbara and her father drove home from Super Hero High in silence. Barbara put her earbuds in, not even bothering to turn on any music. Instead, she stared out the window and watched the city speed past her as she got farther and farther away from Super Hero High.

As the days passed, Barbara could think of nothing but

Principal Waller's invitation to join the student body. When she sat in her French class at Gotham High, her mind was in Doc Magnus's lab, wondering what scientific breakthrough he was teaching. When she was at Super Hero High, adding decibels to Cyborg's sonic blaster or doing her weekly security sweep of the computers, Barbara watched the students laughing and chatting, flying around and playfully zapping one another with their super powers and weapons . . . until hall monitor Hawkgirl shut their antics down.

Barbara noted that the Supers seemed at home with their special skills. Frost chilled a warm soda with a cold puff of air. Beast Boy amused Miss Martian by turning into a frog, then a bat, then back into a boy, in a matter of seconds. Katana sliced through a boring conversation by throwing a sheet of paper into the air and cutting it artfully into a dozen tiny paper doves, which cascaded over Poison Ivy and the other students at their table.

Somehow Barbara now knew this was where she belonged. She was sure of it. At her own school she was often made fun of because she was so smart. Sure, there were a few nice kids there. But at Super Hero High, no one ever mocked another's special abilities. Not even Cheetah or Star Sapphire, who were known to make fun of others behind their backs.

Alone in her room, Barbara tried to come up with ways to address her father's concerns. As police commissioner, he was well aware of the evil that was out there. And as a part-time instructor at Super Hero High, he often told Barbara about the danger the Supers were in. Dinner conversation included stories of mishaps, mistakes, and mayhem, which only fueled her desire to go to Super Hero High.

"Big Barda tossed her Mega Rod so hard it destroyed Parasite's supply shed."

"The Flash was running so fast he crashed into the Vehicle Creation class garage, putting several prototype spacecraft, motorcycles, and cars out of commission."

"Bumblebee got nicked by Supergirl's laser eyes and has sustained an injury."

"Aliens showed up and tried to take over the world . . . *again!*"

"I'd never want anything bad to happen to you, Barbara," her father said one night as he passed the meat loaf. It was one of her favorite dishes. "It would slay me."

Barbara just nodded and played with her mashed potatoes.

Barbara knew she couldn't argue with her dad's feelings. She also knew he couldn't argue with facts. Employing complex computer graphs and charts featuring a matrix of statistics to support her argument and supplemented by state-of-the-art videos, she worked deep into the night.

The next day was Saturday. That afternoon Barbara invited her father into the living room. Her presentation took over an hour, and as Commissioner Gordon sat in his favorite chair nodding, neither smiling nor frowning, Barbara piled fact upon fact and reason upon reason as to why she should be allowed to go to Super Hero High.

"All personality tests confirm that it would be beneficial for me to attend. . . . My test scores would go even higher in the competitive environment. . . . My high-tech skills can help the Supers, and in turn help the world. . . ."

And so on, until finally, when she was done, Barbara smiled. How could her father possibly say no now?

"No," he said. "Babs, you know I'm concerned about your safety. Who will protect you if I'm not around?"

"I can protect myself," she insisted. "You don't trust me!"

"I do trust you," he argued. "It's the criminals and villains I don't trust! And who do super heroes fight? That's right—criminals and villains!"

"Argggggh!" was all Barbara could think of to say. Her father was beyond frustrating. Had he not heard anything she was saying?

"I'm going for a run," she said, heading to the front door.

"Be safe!" her father called after her.

Starting off at a full sprint, Barbara didn't slow until she had gone about a mile. A star athlete as well as a scholar, she wasn't even out of breath. The music on her phone helped her even her pace. In the distance Barbara could see

Mr. Luna's Auto Village and Car Wash. Everyone knew the car dealership with the TV commercials featuring the moon-faced owner shouting, "Mr. Luna moves cars—and cleans them, too!"

On the lot there was an oversized bouncy castle under a canopy of colorful helium balloons to attract customers. As she neared, Barbara could see a handful of kids gleefully jumping up and down inside the castle, laughing and squealing with joy.

Suddenly, the squealing turned to screams. Barbara whipped around, and her eyes grew big at the sight of something wrapping cars in cocoons, some with people still inside them.

"Run!" Mr. Luna shouted, his normally pale face turning redder with each heavy step. "RUN!" he yelled. "It's Killer Moth!!!"

Barbara gasped. From behind a pile of cars, a giant green moth with red wings rose into the air. Wielding a powerful blaster of some sort, he destroyed cars as if they were toys. As he flew toward the bouncy castle, Barbara froze. The children! They were still inside!

In a heartbeat, Barbara ran over to them. "Get out of here," she ordered, helping them down from the castle. "RUN! I'll distract him."

The children were gathered safely in their parents' arms as Barbara climbed to the top of the castle. "Over here!" she yelled to the super-villain. "Come get me!"

Killer Moth jerked his head around, his beady eyes narrowing in on her. He flew toward Barbara, his wings whipping up a windstorm and dislodging all the balloons. Undeterred, Barbara began jumping up and down to gain momentum, then launched herself off the bouncy castle toward the car wash. Killer Moth batted away the balloons and followed as Barbara reached into her micro Utility Belt and took out her tools, tucking a flashlight into her boot. With lightning speed, she reprogrammed the car wash's controls so she could access it through her phone.

"You're looking kind of scruffy!" she yelled to Killer Moth as she stood inside the car wash, daring him to come after her. When he raised his gun, she turned on her high-powered flashlight, knowing that moths were attracted to light, and then flung it onto the car-wash tracks. With Killer Moth momentarily distracted, Barbara picked up a pressure washer hose and knocked the gun out of his hand.

Angered, the insect-villain dived into the tunnel of the car wash. Just as he was about to wrap Barbara in a cocoon, she nimbly leapt aside and pressed a button on her phone. Instantly, a torrent of water from multiple nozzles blasted Killer Moth.

"You're all washed up!" Barbara called. She quickly tied the stunned villain to the conveyor track so that he moved through the tunnel like a car about to get cleaned. "I've programmed the car wash to take care of pesky insects like you!"

Killer Moth was dragged through the first cycle. He was hit by gallons of water from every direction.

"I'll get you!" he growled, as giant rubber scrubbers came down and began to buff him clean. "Hey, I've got soap in my eyes!"

Sirens wailed, getting closer and closer.

The neon FINISHED! sign blinked on and off as Killer Moth came out of the car wash trapped in wax. Never had he looked so squeaky-clean. Mr. Luna and the others broke out in applause as the police swooped in.

"Barbara!" It was her father.

Commissioner Gordon wrapped his daughter in his arms. "I'm so happy you're okay," he said gently. "Killer Moth is a super-villain and doesn't care who he hurts."

"Dad—" Barbara started to say.

"Your safety means the world to me—"

"But, Dad—" she tried again.

"There are bad people out there, Barbara, and I aim to keep you and everyone else as safe as possible."

"Excuse me," Mr. Luna said. His round face was back to its normal color. "Commissioner Gordon, not only can this girl take care of herself, but she saved us all!"

Commissioner Gordon looked around. Everyone was nodding, then began to applaud again as Barbara blushed.

"*Y-you* captured Killer Moth?" her father sputtered.

"Someone had to," she said. "People's lives were in danger. I was just doing what you would have done."

His forehead wrinkled with concern. "I have to deal with that right now," Commissioner Gordon said, pointing to the police van in which Killer Moth was thrashing around. "Barbara, you could have been seriously injured. Or worse. We'll talk tonight when I get home."

CHAPTER 3

That night Barbara made dinner. Spaghetti, her specialty. She added fresh sliced mushrooms from the farmers' market and plenty of crushed garlic—just the way her father liked it. Then she topped it with a generous portion of Parmesan cheese. For dessert: triple chocolate cake from Butterwood's Bakery, something they both loved. She had gotten it to sweeten the deal for her pitch to attend Super Hero High.

Silence settled over the dinner table, neither of them wanting to be the first to speak. Finally, Commissioner Gordon put down his fork and wiped his mouth with a napkin before setting it back down on his lap.

"Delicious dinner." Barbara smiled, but inside she dreaded what he was going to say next. "You could have gotten hurt." Both knew he wasn't talking about the spaghetti.

"You told me that," Barbara reminded him. "But, Dad, I didn't. Instead, I saved a lot of lives."

He nodded slowly.

"You worry about me being able to take care of myself, when I can do even more than that. I can take care of others, too." Barbara's voice began to rise. "You've brought me up to believe that public service is the noblest job a person can have. All I'm asking is to try to be part of that. Training at Super Hero High gives me the best chance in the world to test my skills. Please, Dad, please, can I go?" Barbara stopped. She looked directly at him. "Principal Waller believes in me. Why won't you?"

Her father winced. "I do believe in you, Babs," he said. "I always have. I always will." He exhaled as if he had been holding his breath for years. Perhaps he had been. "Tell you what," he continued, sounding resigned. "You've proven yourself today, so how about we give Super Hero High a chance?"

"POW!" Barbara cheered, leaping from her chair and hugging him tight.

Her father began to chuckle, then said, "If it doesn't pan out, you could be a crisis negotiator. You are certainly persuasive. No, wait—too dangerous."

"DAD! Thank you!" Barbara yelled. She felt as if her heart were going to explode from happiness.

"All right. Calm down," he said. "Of course, there will be a few rules."

Barbara nodded enthusiastically. "Yes, yes, anything!" She could not believe he'd changed his mind!

Her father pulled a notebook from his pocket and began

to write. "You will have a three-month probationary period," he began. "I know there will be bumps and bruises. Super Hero High can be tough at times, with all the physical and weapons training, and I can't keep you out of harm's way completely. However, if at any moment I think you're in real danger, I reserve the right to pull you out and send you right back to Gotham High."

Barbara nodded. That sounded fair. But he wasn't done yet.

"Here are the ground rules," he began as he wrote them down:

1) If you can't handle the workload or your grades drop—you're out.

2) If you develop an attitude—you're out.

3) If you don't keep me informed about everything—you're out.

"Additionally, you are to continue living at home. Even though you may be training to be a super hero, you are still my daughter, and I want you here with me. Is this clear?"

Barbara nodded, unsuccessfully keeping her happiness in check: she was going to Super Hero High!

"Well," her dad said, looking glum. "Is there anything you want to say?"

Barbara lit up. "Yes," she said, looking like she was going

to make some new, even wilder request. The she grinned and added, "Let's have cake!"

Barbara devoured her chocolate cake, but when she reached for a second slice, she noticed that her father hadn't even touched his first piece. What was he so afraid of? she wondered. She'd be just fine—better than fine.

"Barbara reporting to Supergirl. Supergirl, do you read me?"

Her wafer-thin com bracelet crackled before she heard "Oops, ouch! Sorry! Sorry." There was a moment of silence, followed by a loud thud, and then Supergirl's voice came in. "Hey there, BFF. I flew too fast and The Flash was running too fast and we had a major collision. But we're both okay. At least, I think we are. He looks sort of wobbly. What's up?"

Barbara could barely contain herself. "I have big news, but I want to tell you in person."

"I can't wait!" Supergirl said. "See you soon!"

Barbara walked over to her closet. Her heart raced as she took out the simple black costume Katana had made for her. When she slipped into it, she stood taller and felt stronger. She stared at the mirror, not recognizing the girl looking back at her. Who was that? The longer she stared, the more evident it became. Finally, she said in a clear, strong voice, "Barbara Gordon . . . I'd like you to meet Batgirl."

That night, Batgirl had trouble falling asleep. Nights were always a comfort to her, being wrapped in the darkness when the world was quiet. But she had a lot on her mind, naturally. She loved that her best friend, Supergirl, had come up with her super hero name.

Batgirl.

It was perfect. After all, she had her B.A.T.—aka Barbara-Assisted Technology—tech equipment and she loved, loved, loved bats! They were so unassuming and underestimated, flying through the night undetected. Cozy in their caves. She knew bat wings are thinner than bird wings and have more bones, allowing the animals to maneuver more accurately. And because of their echolocation, they can listen to the echoes of sound to locate and identify objects in the dark. How awesome was that?

Batgirl sat on her purple bedspread and looked around the room. There was a poster of Rear Admiral Dr. Grace Murray, who invented the compiler, the program responsible for translating English into computer language. Batgirl hoped that one day she could create a new code or formula that could benefit the world. On another wall were diagrams of space hovercrafts and prototype B.A.T. gadgets and weapons. On her desk were several computers of various sizes and powers, which she had modified herself. And on her nightstand was a framed photo of Barbara sitting on her father's shoulders when she was little. Both had wild, happy smiles.

Batgirl thought about what the next three months would entail. She was an A++ student, but maneuvering through Super Hero High would be the hardest test she had ever taken. She opened her desk drawer and reached past the miscellaneous high-tech tools, wires, and electronic panels, then pulled out a worn red leather diary. On the cover, embossed in gold with stars surrounding the letters, was her name: *Barbara Gordon*. There was a small silver lock on the side. So old-school, but Batgirl loved the quaintness of it. Taking a key from around her neck, she unlocked it.

The first entries were in a childish scrawl. Her father had given her the diary on her seventh birthday. "For important things you want to say or remember," he'd told her.

The first entry read: *Dear Diary, Daddy gave this to me. I am seven now, practically all grown up. But when I'm a real grown-up, I want to be just like him and be a crime fighter!*

As the years passed, there were entries about awards and honors, and slights from others at school. There was misunderstanding and heartbreak. The one thing that remained steady was her determination to fight crime. If anything, this desire grew stronger with each passing year.

Batgirl picked up a pen and looked at the photo of her and her father. Then she turned to a fresh page and wrote:

> Dad has finally agreed to let me attend Super
> Hero High. Now that this is really happening,
> I realize that, in a roundabout way, it is
> something I have dreamed about all my life.
>   I may succeed, I may fail, but I have to try.
> I need to know what I'm made of and how I can
> help make the world a better place. I have the
> best role model in the universe, my father,
> and I hope that one day I can honor him by
> following in his footsteps, fighting crime, evil,
> and injustice.

Despite all her facts and figures, Barbara Gordon is a dreamer—but now Batgirl has the chance to make that dream come true.

She closed the diary and left it on her dresser, along with the key. After all, the diary said *Barbara Gordon* on the cover. She was now Batgirl.

CHAPTER 4

Batgirl whipped around when she heard the crash. Supergirl had flown into the Statue of Justice and was now putting it back on the pedestal. "Is it crooked?" she asked.

"Looks good!" Batgirl said, tilting her head sideways.

Supergirl flew over to her. Her cape fluttered, as did the laces on her red high-tops. Batgirl smiled. Her best friend might have been the strongest person in the world, able to stop comets and missiles and super-bad guys, but she could never remember to tie her shoes.

"What's the big news?" Supergirl's blue eyes sparkled in anticipation.

"Oh," Batgirl said, trying to sound casual. "Not much. It's just that you're looking at THE NEWEST STUDENT AT SUPER HERO HIGH!"

Before she could say anything else, Supergirl was hugging her tight—a little too tight—and jumping up and down.

"You're . . . c-crushing m-m-e!" Batgirl croaked.

"I'm sooooo sorry," Supergirl said, letting her go. "But I'm so excited!"

"Me too," Batgirl said, rubbing her shoulder and laughing.

"Is there some news?" Bumblebee asked as she landed in front of them. She prided herself on being well-informed.

"What's this, a little party?" someone purred. Cheetah was standing nearby watching. Her eyes narrowed.

Katana joined them. "What's going on?" she asked. She unsheathed her sword and casually trimmed the top of an overgrown bush.

Soon Cyborg and The Flash approached, and in a nanosecond, Wonder Woman and Hawkgirl flew over.

"What's happening?" Harley asked as she cartwheeled into the middle of the crowd. She turned on her camera.

"Tell them!" Supergirl squealed. "Batgirl has an announcement!"

Harley beamed as she pushed the camera right into Batgirl's face and yelled, "Action!"

Before the school bell rang, Harley's Quinntessentials already had the scoop. As Harley bounced around, her pigtails springing with each jump, she held the mike and gushed, "Yes, you heard it here first: there's a new hero on the horizon at Super Hero High, and her name is Batgirl!"

"I'll go with you to the principal's office," Supergirl

offered. "Bumblebee can check you in. She works there in the mornings."

Katana examined Batgirl's costume. "If I had known you were going to be wearing this all the time, I'd have made it better," she said.

"It's great the way it is," Batgirl said, adjusting her mask.

Katana flipped her sleek black hair back. "No, I can do better—and I will, in our Intro to Super Suits class!"

Everyone waved to Hawkgirl, who was the hall monitor, and then to Green Lantern, who was using his power ring to carry the monthly care packages his brother had sent him.

A soft buzz got louder as Bumblebee got bigger. Her golden wings stirred the air and she alighted behind the administration office counter. "You're here to see Principal Waller?" she said. She loved being a student assistant and knowing all the buzz about Super Hero High.

Batgirl opened her mouth to speak, but Supergirl beat her to it. "Yes, Batgirl's reporting for her first day as a student at Super Hero High!"

Bumblebee's smile lit up her face. "I know!" she squealed, before remembering that she was working. "I'll need you to fill out the proper paperwork."

Batgirl looked up to see The Wall towering over her. Her dark gray suit and severe haircut matched the serious look she usually wore. "Welcome, Batgirl," Principal Waller said, holding back a smile. "I am so glad your father had a change of heart."

Did my father have a change of heart? Batgirl wondered. Or was he putting her on probation at Super Hero High because it might prove to be too tough for her?

"Thank you. We're so thrilled," Supergirl said.

"I was talking to Batgirl," Waller pointed out. "Supergirl, shouldn't you be somewhere?"

"Huh? Oh! Yes, class. Okay, see you later, *Batgirl!*" Supergirl said before racing down the hallway. She got all the way to the end before turning around, zooming back, and giving Batgirl another hug. Then she finally headed off to join the Supers in Liberty Belle's history class.

"Have a seat, Barbara—I mean, Batgirl," the principal said. "Bumblebee! Oh, you're here?"

Bumblebee handed the principal a folder and winked at Batgirl on her way out.

"Your transcripts from Gotham High School came in, and your grades and test scores are excellent."

Batgirl blushed. She had always been a top student and planned to continue the practice at her new school.

"However," Waller added, "Super Hero High is a very different place from what you're used to."

Batgirl nodded. In the hallways, many of the students used the flight lanes. In PE, instead of running laps around a track, they were often asked to run laps around the city. And in Weaponomics, they were learning about devices that could cause mass destruction—or save the world. As the school's part-time tech wizard, Batgirl had seen it all.

". . . you're here in a different capacity now," Waller was saying. "I want you to cease being our tech whiz and start being a full-time student. Although I may reserve the right to call you in on special assignments."

"I can do both!" Batgirl said. Computers, weapons, electrical, explosive, and incendiary devices: she could start—or stop—them all.

Principal Waller shook her head. "I've already begun looking for your replacement in that department. No, I want you to focus. Because you are a transfer student, you have a lot of catching up to do. This isn't like your old high school. Here, we train students to save lives, make the world a better place, and lead by example. There are villains who will aim to bring you and the world down. We have to be prepared for that."

Batgirl nodded. Her heart was racing. She had wanted this for *so* long.

"Do you have any questions?" Waller asked. She was looking at her telephone—all the buttons were lit up and blinking impatiently.

"Just one," Batgirl said, hesitating. "May I keep my IT annex? The one where I stored all my technical equipment and computers?"

"Of course," Waller said. "Since you'll be commuting to school, it will be good for you to have a place for your things."

Batgirl was relieved that she got to keep her annex, or as she referred to it, her Barbara-Assisted Technology Bunker.

This was also called the Bat-Bunker.

"Thank you. For everything," Batgirl said. "I won't let you down."

"I believe you," Principal Waller said. "But first there's someone I want you to see."

CHAPTER 5

Batgirl knew that every student at Super Hero High had to have an interview with the school counselor, Dr. Arkham. After all, there was a lot of pressure when it came to training to be a super hero. The job was not for everyone.

"He's really nice," Wonder Woman said as Batgirl joined her friends in the dining hall for a late breakfast. She was already digging into her third helping of cereal. Every morning, Wonder Woman lined up seven bowls and worked her way through them until there was not one crunch of cereal left.

Katana sat down with a tray of tropical fruit and, in the blink of an eye, sliced it into beautiful flower shapes. A plate piled high with wheat toast drenched with honey flew overhead and landed on the table as Bumblebee grew to her full size.

Wonder Woman continued, "Dr. Arkham practically invented power naps. Plus, he's written several books, and many of them say the same thing!" Having been homeschooled on Paradise Island before enrolling at Super Hero High, Wonder Woman had a rather interesting view of what life on the rest of the planet was like. A born leader, she was always the first to volunteer for anything. She was forever trying to help Harley Quinn clean and organize her room, not realizing that it was an impossible task.

"You'll do great," Bumblebee assured Batgirl. She had left the crust from her bread on the plate and was licking honey from her thumb and forefinger so it wouldn't go to waste. "We all had to talk to Arkham before becoming students. It's part of the process."

Batgirl stopped mid-chew. She suddenly realized that—yowza!—she was a student now. She had really made it! "What does it take?" Batgirl asked. "You know, to be a super hero?"

"Conviction," Katana said.

"Dedication," Wonder Woman added.

"Strength," Supergirl said, sitting down next to Batgirl.

"Heart," said Poison Ivy.

"Humor!" Harley said, cartwheeling over while eating a bowl of cereal and not spilling a drop of milk.

Soon Supers all across the dining hall were yelling to Batgirl.

"Loyalty!" said Cyborg.

"Flexibility!" Beast Boy offered.

"Money," Star Sapphire interjected.

"Cleverness," Cheetah purred.

"Stealth," Lady Shiva contributed.

"Speed," said The Flash.

"Commitment," said Hawkgirl.

Batgirl smiled, soaking it all in. Everyone's answer was so heartfelt. It made her more excited than ever to be at Super Hero High. She was determined to be all these things and more!

Dr. Arkham stared at her from behind his oversized glasses, then stroked his beard. Batgirl wondered if she would be able to see her reflection in his shiny bald head.

He shuffled through a stack of papers before finding what he was looking for in a purple folder on the floor. Arkham was old-school when it came to technology. Batgirl knew this too well. She had often helped him turn on his computer, shut off his phone, and even open the door when his key got stuck.

"Hmmmm," he said. "Barbara Gordon . . . so now you're Batgirl, is that right?" She nodded. "Your test scores at Gotham High are stellar, and I see that you've never gotten in trouble or even had so much as a tardy slip."

She nodded again.

"So tell me, Ms. Gordon—oh, excuse me! Batgirl!" He chuckled at his own mistake. "Tell me, Batgirl, what makes you think you will do well here? You know you don't have any superpowers, correct?" He leaned forward. "Or do you think you have some?"

"I'm well aware of my capabilities," Batgirl said. "Principal Waller says that you don't have to have superpowers to attend Super Hero High. She says that she's not looking at who you are today, but who you will be in the future."

Dr. Arkham closed the folder and leaned back in his leather chair. It was so big it made him look like a little boy. A bald little boy with a beard.

"I know what she says," he told her. "But I want to hear what you have to say."

Batgirl took a deep breath. How could she tell him what she felt inside? It wasn't logic that was leading her desire to be a super hero, it was her heart.

Arkham was pressing the tips of his fingers together and waiting. Finally, Batgirl said, "It's who I am. It's who I am meant to be. Have you ever just known something deep inside that transcends words? When Principal Waller offered me the opportunity to be a student here, it was as if all the planets aligned and suddenly, for the first time, everything in my life made sense."

Dr. Arkham was silent, his face stoic. Batgirl wondered if she had said the wrong thing. Then she noticed a tear running down his cheek. "Dr. Arkham, are you all right?" she asked.

Momentarily unable to speak, he nodded. Then he said, "Yes, yes, I am, Batgirl. You make more sense than most of the students here. There are things that cannot be measured in a test, like the depth of human emotion. Take me, for example. I am a brilliant counselor and therapist. But I harbor a secret desire to be . . . an opera singer."

To prove this, he stood and belted out strains from *The Marriage of Figaro*. Batgirl marveled at how loud he was. When he was done, Arkham bowed deeply to the four corners of the room. "You have inspired me to take up singing again!"

As he wept with happiness, Batgirl shifted in her chair. "Um, Dr. Arkham," she ventured, "aren't you supposed to give me the other tests?"

"What? Why, yes, yes. Thank you. Yes. Okay!" He held up a card with squiggles on it. "What do you see when you look at this?"

"A knight in armor."

"And this?"

"A bat."

"And this?"

"A whale . . . umm, sorta."

"And this?"

"The battle between good and evil."

By the time they were through, both Batgirl and Dr. Arkham were pleased with the way the session had gone. "One last question," Dr. Arkham said before she left.

Batgirl turned around. "Yes?"

He pulled something out of his desk drawer. "Can you fix my calculator? Instead of adding up the numbers, it just keeps subtracting."

"How did it go? How did it go?" Supergirl asked, eager to hear every little detail. The Super Hero of the Month was always assigned to assist any new students, and Supergirl took her assignment very seriously. Maybe too seriously.

"It went great," Batgirl said as Supergirl accompanied her down the hall.

"Ooh, this room is the forensics computer lab, where they use the latest tech to catch criminals," Supergirl said, pointing like a tour guide.

"I know," Batgirl replied. "Remember, I hooked up all the computers to the server."

"Right!" Supergirl looked delighted that her bestie was already feeling at home. Then she whispered, "Look there, on the wall. That thing that looks like a school bell is really Hawkgirl's hidden radar gun and video camera for catching flyers who break the speed limit in the hall."

Batgirl whispered back, "I know. I installed it for her."

The two friends tried to suppress their giggles as they made their way down the hall.

"Here I am trying to show you around, when you could be

giving me the tour!" Supergirl said as they continued to Doc Magnus's Robotics and Computer Science classroom. "And now for your first official class!" Supergirl announced.

"Thanks," Batgirl said, pushing the door open. "See you at lunch!"

"Later!" Supergirl said, flying away and barely missing Beast Boy, who was running to his class.

"Please, sit up front, Batgirl," Doc Magnus said. "I want to be able to hear whatever insights you have. Your reputation precedes you!"

"That means he likes you," Miss Martian whispered before turning invisible.

"That means you're the teacher's pet," Cheetah said as Batgirl made her way up to the desk with the **RESERVED FOR BATGIRL** sign on it.

Harley turned on her camera and in a loud faux whisper reported, "It's Batgirl's first day of class. Everyone wants to know how this new super hero will fare."

"Camera down, Harley!" Doc Magnus called. "You know the rules. No filming in class."

"Oopsy! I forgot," Harley said, laughing. "Sorry, Doc. Won't happen again."

"Until the next class," Killer Frost said under her breath as she rolled her eyes. Harley stuck out her tongue and returned her attention to the class.

Batgirl was studying Doc Magnus. With advanced degrees in mathematics, particle physics, and mechanical engineering, he was a certified genius—someone she hoped to learn a lot from. His brown hair was cut short, and he wore a purple V-neck sweater with a green blazer and a black tie. Some of the students made fun of the purple he wore every day, but Batgirl understood that habits could be hard to break. She'd also noticed that Doc Magnus was always sucking on a grape lollipop. She wondered if he ever tried other flavors.

Looking around the room, she could see Wonder Woman flipping her hair back, Hawkgirl lining up her pens, and Star Sapphire playing with the violet ring on her finger.

"Who knows the answer?" Doc Magnus was asking with regard to the theoretical physics question he had asked but no one was answering.

Like at Gotham High, Batgirl was always quick to raise her hand.

"Teacher's pet," whispered Catwoman.

"That would be me!" Beast Boy quipped, turning from a green teen to a hamster. He scampered off his desk and onto Catwoman's. She was not amused when he began to nibble on her homework.

Just as she raised a paw and was about to bring it down on him, Beast Boy turned back into a boy and rolled off her desk.

"Temper, temper," he said, blinking innocently as Catwoman seethed. Batgirl smiled, thankful that he'd taken the attention off her.

After school, Lady Shiva, Harley, and Star Sapphire closed in around Batgirl as she waited for her ride home.

"Hi, guys!" she said brightly. She admired Lady Shiva's bright red dress, which never seemed to wrinkle, even when she was practicing her lethal martial arts moves.

"Oh, there you are," Star Sapphire said, handing Batgirl her phone. She adjusted her glittering gemstone necklace. "My phone's a mess. I have too many friends and fans sending me messages all the time. It takes forever to download anything, and Daddy's IT support is hopeless with even the simplest requests. Can you reprogram this so it's faster? Oh, and I'd like it back this afternoon."

"Can you come to my room?" Harley asked. "My camera is acting weird."

"I need a custom computerized spreadsheet for my mathematical calculations," Lady Shiva said.

"Well, technically, I'm not in the tech department anymore," Batgirl began. They all stared at her blankly. "But sure!" she said. "I'd be happy to help."

"Hey," Katana said, breaking up the circle. "That's not Batgirl's job. She's here to be a student, just like the rest of us."

"Says who?" Star Sapphire challenged her.

"Says me," Supergirl interjected brightly. "I'm supposed

to take care of her and help her adjust."

"Hey! Whoa," Batgirl interrupted as the group bickered. "I can help until the new tech person is hired," she insisted.

Everyone stopped talking and stared at her.

"What?" Batgirl asked. "Have I ever let you down before? I can do this!"

Supergirl bit her lip and Star Sapphire looked triumphant.

"It's okay," Batgirl assured her best friend. "I'm going to be fine."

She felt a wave of relief when Supergirl broke into a smile. "Of course you are!" she said. "I should never doubt you!"

Katana didn't look so sure, but she nodded.

"Great!" Harley said, somersaulting away. "See ya later!"

As Batgirl watched her friends disappear into the high school, a car horn startled her. It was her dad. Her first day had been incredibly exciting, but she had a lot of catching up to do in each class. *She could do it all, right?*

CHAPTER 6

As the days turned into a week, and then beyond, breakfasts at home got weird. Or rather, weirder. Batgirl and her father didn't talk about Super Hero High. The subject seemed to be a dark cloud hanging over them. In the past, Barbara had shared everything about school, and she loved hearing Commissioner Gordon discuss his detective work.

The two still talked, of course. But it was mostly about the weather and other safe subjects. Except when the weather was menacing—then her dad got overprotective and insisted that she take an additional raincoat, umbrella, poncho, rain boots, *and* her long raincoat, just in case the other raincoat and the poncho weren't enough to keep her dry. But discussion about her new life as a Super was off-limits. Whenever Batgirl tried to bring it up, her father would make some weak excuse, like, "Whoa, I forgot to polish my shoes. Better do it now before I forget again!" And then he'd excuse himself.

If it was a Tuesday or Thursday, his teaching days, Batgirl got a ride to school in the police car. The other days, she took the Gotham Line to the Metropolis Metro, then transferred to a bus that delivered her in front of the iconic Amethyst Tower of Super Hero High. With just a few steps, she was back in the thick of her new routine.

"Crazy Quilt lets us come up with our own extra-credit projects," Katana told her as they made their way down the hall. Both ducked when a large and unusually animated snapdragon came snaking wildly in their direction.

"Sorry!" Poison Ivy called, chasing the unruly plant. Her cheeks flushed the color of her red hair. The snapdragon kept snapping at Supers as it brushed past them, occasionally snagging a book or swallowing a backpack.

Katana continued as if nothing had happened. Her focus was legendary. "I'm making *you* my extra-credit project," she announced as Cyborg came barreling toward them. He skidded to a stop in front of Batgirl and stood awkwardly, blocking her path.

"Hey, Barb . . . um, Batgirl," he said. "I'm so sorry, but I think I need a minor adjustment."

Batgirl knew Cyborg, who was part boy, part computer, really well. In the past, she'd served as his tech troubleshooter whenever he malfunctioned, which was often. She reached for the micro tool kit in her Utility Belt, and with a simple adjustment to his internal circuitry, he was good to go.

Batgirl didn't mind when Cyborg asked for help. He was a computer and electronics expert himself. She found it comforting to have a friend whose eyes didn't glaze over when she mentioned kilobytes, digital integrated circuits, and mega metadata. So many Supers took their special skills and powers for granted. But Batgirl was always on the cutting edge, constantly learning and updating her technology.

To fall behind could mean the difference between success and defeat.

Batgirl had always loved school. Whether studying a new math formula, an historical treaty, or a computer program, she enthusiastically jumped right in. So it was no surprise that she sought to study her fellow Supers. After all, if she was to fit in and succeed at Super Hero High, what better role models did she have?

As Batgirl observed her peers, she was amazed that the social interactions were not all that different from the ones at Gotham High. There were the leaders, like Wonder Woman. The sometimes snobbish, like Star Sapphire. The rule followers (and enforcers), like Hawkgirl. The optimists, like Bumblebee. The jocks, like The Flash. The artists, like Katana. The goofballs, like Beast Boy. The naturalists, like Poison Ivy. The introverts, like Miss Martian. The extroverts, like Harley. And the teachers' pets, like . . . well, like her.

Doc Magnus was always praising Batgirl in class, which she found embarrassing. Other teachers were impressed by Batgirl, too. She was acing Super Hero History, and in Weaponomics, Mr. Fox was quick to point out that Batgirl could turn an ordinary object like a bottle opener into a functional weapon. PE, however, was another story.

Wildcat, their phys ed teacher, stood with his hoodie up and a clipboard in his paw. "Go! Go! Go!" he yelled out every three seconds. With each "Go!" someone took off. Batgirl watched in awe as Hawkgirl, then Super Girl, then Bumblebee, then Wonder Woman all shot into the sky and flew laps around the school.

When it was her turn, Batgirl stood poised at the starting line.

"Go!"

She was off, running as fast as she could. Soon someone was passing her. "See ya!" Cheetah said, smiling.

"I got this!" Harley said, running backward, then doing a couple of flips while still holding her camera.

"Why be a boy when you can be a gazelle?" Beast Boy asked, turning into one and gracefully galloping ahead.

And so it went until every Super had passed her.

"Three minutes and nineteen seconds," Wildcat grunted, clicking his stopwatch. "Not bad."

Not good, either, Batgirl thought, crossing the finish line last. She knew that with no superpowers, she was going to have to be in top physical shape.

"Um, Supergirl," she began, her attention drawn away for a moment as Green Lantern and Star Sapphire walked off, comparing their glowing power rings *again*. "How are you adjusting—you know, to life on Earth . . . Super Hero High?"

"Fine, thank you." Supergirl tied her shoelaces. "How are *you* doing, Batgirl?"

"Fine, too, I guess," Batgirl said, not too convincing.

"Why? What? What's the matter?" Supergirl felt her forehead. "You're not sick, are you? I'm supposed to help you adjust. Are you having a problem? Oh, wow. You're having a problem, aren't you? Do you want to talk about it? Or see Dr. Arkham? Let's go see him right now! Together."

Batgirl laughed and put her hands on Supergirl's shoulders. "Dr. Arkham's great," she said. "But what I really need is to talk to you, bestie."

Supergirl slowed down. "I would love that," she said. "Capes and Cowls Café?"

"Capes and Cowls!" Batgirl agreed.

As always, Capes & Cowls Café in downtown Metropolis was busy. There were students from Super Hero High, CAD Academy, and Metropolis High, sometimes at their own tables, sometimes sharing one. The cozy couches and board games gave the place a homey feel, yet the awesome color scheme and energetic vibe made this the trendy place to be.

"Hi, Supergirl!" the server said. When Steve Trevor smiled, his silver braces glistened. "Is Wonder Woman going to join you?"

Batgirl noticed his grin waver slightly when Supergirl said she was not.

"But I do want to introduce you to Batgirl!" Supergirl said. "She's new to our school."

"Nice to meet you, Batgirl," Steve said as the two shook hands.

Batgirl looked away, pretending to be interested in Hawkgirl and Poison Ivy at a nearby table. They looked like they were telling secrets. Would Steve recognize her? Batgirl wondered. As Barbara Gordon, she frequented the café after she had completed her tech assignments and to do her own homework. Their strawberry smoothies were the best.

"Batgirl?" Steve repeated, staring at her. She looked back at him, happy to be wearing her mask and hoodie. "Can I ask you something?"

"Yes, um. Sure," she said. "What is it?"

"I hesitate to say this, but . . ."

Batgirl gulped—*Oh, capes! He recognizes me!*

". . . that's my order pad you're holding."

Batgirl looked at her hands and started laughing. Sure enough, she had picked up Steve's pad by mistake and was crumpling it.

"So sorry," she said, still laughing with relief. "Here you go!"

"Um, okay," he said, backing away. "Just let me know when you two are ready to order."

"The usual," Supergirl said. "Thanks, Steve."

Batgirl watched as some boys from CAD Academy called him over. Before she could warn him, Captain Cold pulled out his cold gun and created a slick of ice on the floor. When Steve slipped and fell, their table erupted in laughs.

Batgirl hurried to help him up, but Supergirl got there first.

"I'm fine," Steve said. His face was bright red.

"That wasn't nice," Batgirl said to Captain Cold.

"Who are you?" Captain Cold asked, looking her up and down. Ratcatcher, his vile-looking buddy, snickered.

"I'm Batgirl," she said, meeting his glare. It felt weird to be saying that in public.

"Gnat Girl?" Captain Cold sneered.

Batgirl felt an icy chill go through her entire body.

"*Ice* to meet you," Captain Cold said. If he weren't so

mean, he might be handsome, with his square jaw and piercing blue eyes.

Batgirl pressed the heat button on her Batsuit to get her temperature back to normal.

Captain Cold looked at Steve. "Hope you had a nice trip. See you next *fall*," he quipped.

Ratcatcher let out a high-pitched laugh. *Could he be more annoying?* Batgirl wondered.

"Come on, Batgirl," Supergirl said, pulling her away. "Let's not waste our time with these two."

"Smart thinking," Batgirl said.

They returned to their table to find that their order had arrived. As the two sipped smoothies, Batgirl confided, "School is harder than I thought it would be."

"I know!" Supergirl said. "The tests are so hard!"

"Well, not those so much as learning to navigate the social circles."

Supergirl played with her straw and nodded. "Less than a year ago, I was at school on Krypton, my home planet. I knew everyone there. I had grown up with them. And then suddenly, I find myself at Super Hero High. And with powers I couldn't even imagine! I'm still trying to adjust."

Batgirl took another sip of her smoothie. She liked that Steve used fresh strawberries. "But at least you have powers," she said. "I'm just a regular girl."

Supergirl laughed so hard that after a while no sound came out. Catching her breath, she gasped and said, "Batgirl, you are anything but *regular*. You're smarter than anyone I know, and you can fix and make anything."

"Thanks, Supergirl," said Batgirl. She wanted to talk about her dad, but she remembered that both Supergirl's parents had perished on Krypton when the planet exploded. Suddenly, she felt silly for feeling sorry for herself. "I'm so glad we're best friends."

"Me too," Supergirl said. "We make a great team!"

Katana slid into an empty seat at their table. "Beast Boy is at it again," she said.

They looked over to see him showing some kids from Metropolis High how he could turn into a grasshopper, then leaping from table to table.

"I can turn into anything!" Beast Boy boasted when he was back to his normal green self.

Batgirl watched Katana fold, then slice her napkins into paper warriors. She watched Supergirl lift the refrigerator so Steve could retrieve a lemon that had rolled under it. She sighed. Barbara Gordon had always been herself: smart, techy, athletic . . . normal. Barbara Gordon didn't know any other way of being. But Batgirl realized that she needed to step up her game if she was to compete with flyers, shape-shifters, and mind readers. But how?

Batgirl looked around the room and smiled. The answer was all around her.

CHAPTER 7

"**H**igher!" Katana commanded. They were outside on the grass near the Amethyst Tower. "Higher, and hold it like you mean it!"

Batgirl gripped the sword and tried to mimic Katana's battle stance. Always resourceful, Batgirl had realized that she was surrounded by superheroes, so why not take advantage of that? For martial arts training, she had enlisted the granddaughter of the world's first female samurai super hero. Katana had been drilling her in basic sword moves and stances for the last half hour.

"Thanks so much!" Batgirl said as they parried back and forth.

"No, thank *you!*" Katana lowered her voice. "I'm hoping to become the fencing team captain, and one of the responsibilities is to help train the team. This is great practice for me, too! Now it's time to move on to your roundhouse kicks and punches."

Batgirl set the sword down. It was heavier than it looked. She bent down to touch her toes for a stretch, but before she could stand, she heard, "Block!"

Instinctively, Batgirl blocked Katana's swift roundhouse kick. Soon the two girls were sparring. Batgirl weaved back and forth and bobbed up and down to avoid getting pummeled.

"Come at me harder!" Katana instructed. "Don't be afraid to show your strength."

They sparred ferociously until Katana got Batgirl in a headlock, by which time a crowd had gathered, cheering for them.

"Oomph!" Batgirl said, her voice sounding muffled. "Thank you!"

"You're welcome," Katana said, letting her go and giving her a deep bow. "Tomorrow, we'll work more on your kicks. Be sure to do a hundred squats tonight, then a hundred more."

Before Batgirl had a chance to rest, Harley came cartwheeling over. "My turn!" she said, leaping up, swinging around a tree branch, and sticking her landing. "You ready for this?"

Batgirl looked surprised. Was it already time for Harley's gymnastics lesson? She took a deep breath and nodded. All her life, Batgirl had wanted to learn from the best, and now she was doing exactly that. Still, it was daunting. Her friends and classmates were willing to give her their time and help with their specialties, but that didn't make it any easier.

As the afternoon wore on, Harley coached her in gymnastics; then The Flash ran with her around the school, giving her tips along the way—"Remember to breathe!"

Arrowette was in charge of archery training. "Focus! Batgirl, focus!" Arrowette commanded, taking a gleaming arrow out of the quiver on her back. "Watch and learn."

Batgirl's jaw dropped when Arrowette effortlessly pulled back her bow and released. The arrow soared, cutting through the sky with a sound like metal being sliced. It ripped through the stem of an apple hanging on a tree, and before the apple hit the ground, Beast Boy caught it.

"Thanks for the snack, Arrowette!" he called as he walked away happily munching.

"Arrowette says it's all about the aim," Batgirl told Big Barda later.

"It's all about the punch," Barda told her. "Like this!" Batgirl tried not to flinch when Barda hit a padded target so hard it flew across the workout room. "Now you try!"

Batgirl made a fist, pulled it back, and struck hard. The target barely moved.

"Again!" Barda barked.

Batgirl hit it again, and again, and again.

Barda sighed. "You're pretty strong, but you can't toss

cars or push over buildings," she said.

"It's not all about strength," Batgirl noted. "I'm pretty agile, and I have my weapons, gadgets, and gear."

"Yeah, yeah," Barda said, adjusting the belt around her yellow costume. "But when you meet new people, you should always hit them hard, and if that doesn't work, hit them harder. Remember to always lead with a punch. BOOM!"

"When I meet someone new, I prefer to lead with a smile," Batgirl said, offering her one.

Barda looked at her with suspicion. Batgirl knew that Barda was fairly new at the school, having been recruited by Vice Principal Grodd. As a former member of the evil Granny Goodness's Female Furies, Barda had once tried to destroy Super Hero High. And now, here she was a student at that same school.

"Are you trying to mess me up?" Big Barda asked. Her fists were clenched.

Batgirl shook her head. "I'm trying to be your friend," she said.

"Why?" Barda asked. Her eyes narrowed. "You know what people around here think of me."

"I know what *I* think of you. And why wouldn't I want to be your friend?" Batgirl said. "My father says that everyone deserves a second chance. That's when you see what people are really made of. Besides, when I see you, I think of who you will be tomorrow."

Barda looked curious, so Batgirl continued. "A lot of kids

around here remember me as Barbara Gordon, hired help. Tech whiz from Gotham High. They can't imagine me as one of them, a future super hero. Can you?"

Barda's face grew serious, but what she did next took Batgirl's breath away. She smiled. Big Barda had the most beautiful smile Batgirl had ever seen. Her entire face lit up.

"Wow!" Batgirl said. "You should do that more often!"

Barda blushed, then frowned. "Don't get too used to it," she growled. But Batgirl noticed that when Barda walked away, a hint of a smile returned.

CHAPTER 8

The teachers at SHH were as supportive as the students. Each one was determined to help turn Batgirl into the best super hero she could be.

"Did you see the article Lois Lane wrote?" Doc Magnus asked as he plucked a metal leaf from his hair.

"Not yet," she said.

Batgirl was helping him clean up after class. One of Poison Ivy's robotic plants had exploded, and thorns and leaves were everywhere. Batgirl was using an old-fashioned magnet to pick them up.

"Well," Doc Magnus said, looking pleased. "She interviewed me, and when she asked who my most promising student is this year, I said you!"

"Oh. Thank you!" Batgirl said. "But there are so many great Supers here."

"Yes, but you have special skills in science and robotics that I have not seen before. Batgirl, you are poised to be a leader in the tech field!" he told her.

"Um, does my dad know how you feel?" she asked.

"Yes, yes," Doc Magnus assured her. "I told him that you are a prodigy and that I am thrilled to have you as a student."

Batgirl nodded again. If only her father were as proud of her as her Robotics teacher.

In Weaponomics, Mr. Lucius Fox strolled past Batgirl, then backed up to watch her. She was putting the finishing touches on a B.A.T. bola—four lengths of reinforced ropes with metal balls on the end that could be thrown to ensnare a villain's arms, legs, or whole body.

"Let's see if this works, shall we?" Mr. Fox said, looking around the room. "I need a volunteer. Beast Boy? You'll do!"

"Huh? Wha—" Beast Boy began. But before he could finish his sentence, Batgirl had flung the bola so that it wrapped around him, pinning his arms to his sides.

"Good job!" Mr. Fox said cheerily as Star Sapphire accidentally-on-purpose poked Beast Boy. He wobbled and fell over with a thud.

When Batgirl ran over to help him up, the floor turned to ice and she slipped and fell.

"Oopsie! My bad," Killer Frost said.

"Leave her alone," Cyborg ordered. "It's not her fault she's smarter than you."

"Oh, ouch!" Frost said. "Looks like someone needs a bodyguard."

Batgirl ignored them as they began to bicker, instead helping Beast Boy up and apologizing.

Later, in PE, Batgirl approached Cyborg. "Hey," she said, "thanks for defending me, but you don't have to do that."

"I don't mind," Cyborg assured her. "That's what friends are for." Even though half of his head was metal and robotic parts, his face was expressive.

Batgirl cleared her throat. "Okay. Um, let me phrase this another way: Please don't defend me. While I appreciate it, I need to fight my own battles."

Cyborg's red cybernetic eye gleamed mischievously. "Okay. Sure," he said. "I thought I was helping. You know I've got your back if you ever need it."

"Back atcha," Batgirl replied just as Wildcat called out, "Students, all eyes on me! Today is gonna be rough!"

Everyone groaned. Wildcat had a reputation for being tough. Fair, but tough.

Batgirl stretched and flexed her muscles. She knew that this class would be harder than Weaponomics or Robotics. It would be the real challenge. The good thing was that Batgirl always relished a challenge.

But an hour and several exhausting maneuvers later . . .

"Ooooh, ouch! I thought I was in great shape," Batgirl groaned as she left Wildcat's class. She could barely walk. Her legs felt like jelly from all the squats and sprints, and her arms hung by her sides as if bereft of muscles. At least now was free period. She could use a little rest with her friends.

"You are so strong," Batgirl noted as she watched Wonder Woman help knock down an old concrete wall some construction workers were demolishing.

"Thank you!" Wonder Woman said as she dusted off her hands.

"Yes, well, a lot of you are super-strong," Batgirl noted. "But I can barely lift the tires Wildcat had me throw."

"It is hard," Bumblebee agreed as she joined them. They were gathered under the shade of a flowering tree. Poison Ivy flung open a blanket and placed it on the ground. In the time it had taken Bumblebee to hand Batgirl a warm cup of honey-lemon tea, lightning-fast Supergirl had gone to fetch the picnic basket filled with fresh fruits and veggies, and butter cookies from her aunt Martha.

"All of us have different skills," Bumblebee continued. "I may not be able to lift a house, but I can stop a train with my Electrical Stings."

"And I can call on the plants to aid me," Poison Ivy volunteered.

"That's right," Wonder Woman said. "And you have us to back you up if you need muscles."

To prove her point, she leapt up and flexed her biceps,

and the others joined in. Batgirl laughed at their bodybuilder poses, and soon everyone was cracking up.

"Well, if anyone needs any tech or weapons or gadgets, I'm your girl!" Batgirl said, warming to the idea that they each had their talents.

"Actually, I do," said Star Sapphire. Batgirl was surprised. She hadn't realized she was listening. "This could use a microcomputer. Think you could have that done for me in two days?"

Batgirl looked at the diamond-encrusted watch. "Well, I'm pretty busy, but . . ." Sapphire looked at her and played with the ring on her finger. Suddenly Batgirl felt a wave of camaraderie wash over her. "Sure, sure. Yes, I'll get right on it!" she heard herself say.

By the time Crazy Quilt's class rolled around, Batgirl was feeling the full effect of Wildcat's PE exercises. Every muscle she had, even some she didn't know she had, was sore.

"Hello! Hello! Hello!" Crazy Quilt cried. He raised his arms high above his head and struck a dramatic pose. Batgirl admired his retro fashion sense. She knew of no one else who would have put together an ensemble of dark flared cords with a white belt, a multicolored polyester vest, a puffy purple pirate shirt and an ascot, and pointy shoes.

"Today is *your* day," Crazy Quilt continued. "I'm turning

the class over to one of my students! Katana? Katana, where are you?"

She stood up in the back of the room.

"Up here! Up, up, up! Join Crazy Quilt and tell the class what your plans are for today's lesson!"

Katana was dressed in black and gray with a slash of red and lace-up cream-colored boots. Batgirl admired how she managed to look regal yet chic and sporty at the same time.

"As you know, I helped create Batgirl's costume," Katana told the class. Batgirl felt all eyes on her. "And while it is functional, I feel that it's not complete. Today, I'd like us all to contribute ideas as to how we can make it better, like adding some deep purple for depth of color and finessing the hoodie. Of course, Batgirl and I will have the final say. Batgirl"—Katana beckoned—"please join me up front."

Crazy Quilt clapped, causing a pedestal to rise in the center of the room. As an introvert, Batgirl was not comfortable with a lot of attention. But that was exactly what she was getting as her fellow Supers walked around her, taking notes and talking. Crazy Quilt encouraged them, saying things like "Form and function!" and "Fun and fighting!"

"Wings!" Beast Boy suggested.

"She can't fly," Sapphire pointed out.

"But I can," Batgirl said, whipping out her grappling hook, throwing it over an air-conditioning pipe overhead, and swinging across the room. "Plus, I'm working on a jetpack and wings."

"Show-off," she heard Cheetah growl quietly.

"See?" Katana said. "Her costume must be able to easily accommodate all her weapons and whatnots."

Katana was so busy getting input from the class that there was one person whose opinion was left out. "Would anyone else like to add anything?" she finally said.

"Ahem."

Everyone looked up to the girl standing on the pedestal. "I have something to add."

Katana blushed. "Of course!" she said. "Yes, Batgirl."

"Well, I love what I've heard everyone say, but I do have one request."

Crazy Quilt nodded. "Yes, yes, go ahead. This is your costume, and it should reflect who you are. Most importantly, you need to feel comfortable in it. Everyone, shush. Let's listen to what Batgirl has to say!"

Batgirl felt her cheeks flush. "Well, I love that several of you suggested sleek titanium boots." Arrowette and Green Lantern nodded knowingly. "But I'd like to keep my plain old leather boots. They're what I'm comfortable in and, well, this . . ."

There was a gasp in the room as Batgirl leapt down from the pedestal, and before she landed, her boots lifted her up again using a hidden spring coil. Then, midair, she flipped over, thanks to Harley Quinn's training, and let her heels attach her to the ceiling so she was hanging upside down. Batgirl was relieved that the suction vacuum grippers she had bought on sale were working.

"Got it!" Harley yelled. She turned the camera on herself. "A Harley Quinntessential exclusive once again."

Still upside down, Batgirl waved to the class as Crazy Quilt led the applause. Just then, Bumblebee flew into the room holding a pink slip of paper. Everyone held their breath. A pink slip meant someone was being called to Principal Waller's office.

"Oh!" Bumblebee said. "Sorry, I thought Batgirl was in this class."

Batgirl felt her boots loosening from the ceiling. With an unceremonious fall, she hit the ground, hurting both her head and her pride.

"Here I am," Batgirl said weakly.

"Batgirl," Bumblebee said, helping her up. "You're wanted in Principal Waller's office. And hurry."

PART TWO

CHAPTER 9

As Bumblebee flew to the principal's office, Batgirl jogged alongside her, still aching from PE class and now nursing a big bump on her head.

"Am I in trouble?" Batgirl asked as they approached the admin office.

"Can't say," Bumblebee said, slowing down and winking at her.

Batgirl could hear two voices coming out of Principal Waller's office. She knocked on the door before pushing it open.

"Ah! Here she is now!" Principal Waller exclaimed.

A woman wearing a tall, exquisite green hat topped with a plume of purple feathers turned around. Batgirl could smell her flowery perfume.

"Hello, dear," the woman said, extending her manicured hand. Her nail polish matched her hat. She spoke quickly, as if her words might run out before she could say them all. "You probably already know me. I'm Alicia Chen of Alicia Chen TV Productions, Inc."

Batgirl smiled politely. The name sounded familiar.

Alicia continued. "My company produces the top reality shows in the country, and we are currently in production for the pilot of a new one." She smiled, clearly pleased with what she was about to say next. "It's called . . . *TechTalkTV*!"

Alicia Chen paused, waiting for a reaction. When she didn't get one, she said again, "*TechTalkTV,* an Alicia Chen TV production!"

"Oh," Batgirl said, wondering why she was being told this. "That sounds exciting."

"YES! Yes, it is," Alicia enthused. "And the excitement continues right here at Super Hero High. Do you know why?"

Batgirl shook her head.

"Because," Alicia announced, "YOU HAVE BEEN SELECTED TO BE ON THE SHOW!"

When Batgirl didn't respond, Alicia patted her on the head. "I know, I know, dear. You're in shock. 'Me?' you're asking yourself. 'Why me on this prestigious TV pilot?' Well, here's why: we scoured the country for the top minds in high-tech, and the chatter was that there's a new top tech super hero at Super Hero High. When we contacted your Robotics teacher, Doc Magnus, he raved about you! *R-A-V-E-D!*

"*TechTalkTV* is a new high-tech competition—a live

show designed to identify the most technically savvy people around. If the pilot scores, this show will be an annual event, like the Super Bowl, only bigger!"

Batgirl nodded. She was never one to blurt out what she thought, unlike Harley or some of the others. As Alicia Chen batted her thick eyelashes, Batgirl said, "Thank you. I'm really flattered. But I'm not sure I'm the right person for the competition."

"But you fit the demographic perfectly!" the producer insisted. "Plus, you can back it up with your tech skills! And you have not just brains, but beauty, too! Look at you! Your big green eyes. That long auburn hair. That perky nose."

"Thank you," Batgirl said, blushing. "But right now my focus is on my studies. I don't want my training to get sidetracked."

Batgirl looked at Waller for help. "This is your call," the principal said to Batgirl. "I will support your decision either way."

Undeterred, Alicia Chen rose to let herself out. "Oh, one more thing. Did I mention that there's a big cash prize for the winner?"

Batgirl touched the bump on her forehead. It still hurt from when she'd fallen from the ceiling because she had used bargain-basement equipment.

"Think about it," the producer said. "Think hard, Batgirl. This could be a game changer."

Later that afternoon, thanks to Bumblebee, everyone had heard that famous TV producer Alicia Chen was on campus.

"Why didn't she have a meeting with me?" Harley demanded, pouting. She hit a stump with her mallet, sinking it flat into the ground.

Wonder Woman flew across the flight track at top speed, followed closely by Supergirl, who, in an effort to overtake her, slammed into the cushioned wall.

"Dial it down!" Supergirl scolded herself. "Hey, Wonder Woman, what are we talking about?"

"Batgirl's been invited to be on national TV to showcase her tech savvy," Wonder Woman reminded her as the two flew back to the starting line. "How awesome is that? This could be big for Super Hero High!"

Batgirl pretended not to hear them as she logged their stats into the computer. The entire solar system was aware that Wonder Woman had led their school to victory in the 100th Super Triathlon. All the media channels had pegged Super Hero High as *the* school for super heroes, and as Harley was fond of saying, "Any publicity is good publicity, but good publicity is even better good publicity!"

Supergirl put her hand on Batgirl's shoulder. "How do you feel about this?" she asked. "What does your heart say?

What is your brain telling you? What do *you* want to do?"

Miss Martian suddenly materialized. "You know what you want to do," she said. "But whether you'll do it is what you are trying to decide."

Batgirl couldn't argue with that. After all, not only could Miss Martian make herself invisible, she could also read minds, which meant that lots of times when Supers saw her coming, they ran away looking guilty. Before Batgirl could respond, Miss Martian was gone. Or was she?

"Why *wouldn't* you do it?" Lady Shiva asked, jumping into the conversation.

"Maybe she's afraid she's going to fail?" Cheetah purred.

Katana joined the group. "She's not going to fail," she assured them. "Batgirl isn't afraid of anything!"

While everyone debated whether she should be on the show, Batgirl slipped away to her Bat-Bunker, logged on to her computer, and began making a list:

CONS

- Don't want to.
- Don't want the publicity.
- Don't want to show off.
- Don't want to fail.

PROS

- Brings recognition to Super Hero High.
- Could pay for B.A.T. tech supplies.
- Could be fun?
- Nice to meet other tech-savvy techsters.

Batgirl continued adding to the list, assigning each item a number 1, 2, or 3, reflecting how important it was. Then, at last, she pressed a button and ran the numbers. She nodded when the computer gave her the answer her mind had already calculated.

Yep. That seemed about right.

It was hard to keep a secret at Super Hero High, and soon everyone knew that Batgirl was going to compete on *TechTalkTV*.

The next day, the Junior Detective Society members cornered Batgirl in the hallway after Liberty Belle's history class. As students flew, skated, raced, and rolled past them, The Flash spoke up. "It's totally cool that you're going to be on the *TechTalkTV* show. We want to help!"

Hawkgirl closed her wide wings to give passersby a wider berth. "We can find out who your competitors are," she offered.

"That would be helpful, right?" Poison Ivy asked. She pushed a batch of spotted black beckoning begonias back into her backpack when they threatened to escape.

Batgirl had often admired the synergy the trio had and wished she were a Junior Detective. After all, she loved mysteries and had often helped her father close cases—at least, she used to. Still, she didn't want the Junior Detective

Society members to think she needed help. After all, tech was her specialty. Did they think she couldn't handle things on her own?

"Thank you," Batgirl said. "But I'll run an analysis to see if I can come up with who's on the list."

"Oh, okay," Poison Ivy said, trying to keep the smile on her face.

"Well, if you need any help, we're here," Hawkgirl assured her.

"You don't want our help?" The Flash asked, surprised.

"I'm fine on my own," Batgirl assured them. "I'm used to going solo when it comes to tech."

That was true. Most evenings she was alone with her computers and equipment. And before she was a student at Super Hero High, Supers came to her for tech help, not the other way around.

As Batgirl made her way to the Bat-Bunker, someone whispered loudly, "Psssst!"

It was Harley.

"Pssssssssst!!!" she hissed so loudly that Green Lantern bumped into Miss Martian, who turned invisible before he could apologize. "The Internet is abuzz with the names of *TechTalkTV* competitors," Harley proclaimed. "I've got a list of potentials. Don't ask me how I got it! Okay, okay, I'll tell you: Alicia Chen leaked it herself! It's great publicity. She's a genius! Of course you're on the list, but look who else is there!"

Once inside the Bat-Bunker, Batgirl input the names of the one hundred possibilities into her computer. She took her own name off the list to reduce the variables. On another monitor she could hear Harley teasing, "Who will be on *TechTalkTV*'s pilot show? I know. Do you?"

Batgirl turned down the volume so she could focus. Before long, using complex analytics, demographics, and Internet rumors, she narrowed down the list. As she stared at it, she took a deep breath. In the world of high tech, these were indeed powerhouses.

"We all want to help," Supergirl began. Several of Batgirl's friends had gathered with her in Wonder Woman's room.

"Here at Super Hero High, we're a team," Wonder Woman jumped in.

"I can help you with public relations and interviewing," Harley volunteered. "TV pointers. I can teach you how to project your voice. How to lower it for dramatic effect."

Batgirl had never considered this. She relished taking tests, but they had all been written, not on television, and certainly not before a live TV audience. No one was sure what the *TechTalkTV* competition would entail, but Alicia Chen's shows were famous for their surprises. Batgirl hoped she wouldn't have to eat bugs.

"I can quiz you," Supergirl said. "Ask you all sorts of tech-y questions. I might not know the answers, but Doc Magnus said he would give me lists to ask you."

"I can serve as your overall coach," Wonder Woman volunteered. "To encourage you and help with morale."

As Bumblebee, Hawkgirl, Katana, Poison Ivy, and others told Batgirl how they could help, she felt a lump in her throat. They really and truly wanted her to do the best she could.

"It's okay to have help," Miss Martian said shyly, having read her mind. "In fact, it's not just you who benefits. It's all of us. At Super Hero High, we work together."

"Wait! Don't disappear," Batgirl begged. "Thank you."

Miss Martian smiled back. Her green cheeks blushed, but she stayed in the room.

CHAPTER 10

Supergirl tugged on Batgirl's sleeve and led her to a table where Big Barda was sitting alone. "Let's sit here," she said, putting down her tray. It was piled high with corn on the cob, a mountain of mashed potatoes, and fried chicken.

"May we join you?" Batgirl asked Barda.

Big Barda shrugged and continued chewing on a roll and not looking happy. Batgirl wasn't sure if it was the roll, the fact that she and Supergirl wanted to sit with her, or something else entirely that was making her look like that.

Cheetah was carrying her tray high above her head with one hand and had her books in the other. "She a friend of yours?" she asked, not even attempting to hide her smirk. "'Cause I hear Big Barda is bad news."

"She's *good* news!" Supergirl said.

"You don't know that," Cheetah said. Others nearby nodded as Catwoman slipped some silverware into the backpack she had just picked up earlier that day. "I'd be careful around her! She can't be trusted."

"I can hear you," Big Barda said, locking eyes with Cheetah.

"You should give her a chance," Batgirl interjected.

"I don't have to give her anything." Cheetah sniffed. "I don't trust her!"

Several of the Supers around her began nodding, but Batgirl did not.

Barda got up and stormed out of the dining hall.

"See, she's a bit unhinged," Cheetah said, smiling sweetly.

"We all make mistakes," Supergirl called to Barda as she and Batgirl followed the girl down the hall. "But you're turning your life around. I admire that!"

"You're probably the only one," Barda said. She crossed her arms and leaned against her locker, glaring at the passing students as if daring them to say something.

"Everything okay?" Hawkgirl asked, landing in front of them.

"We're fine," Supergirl assured her.

"Well, I'm glad you're here," Batgirl told Barda. "You've been a great help teaching me fighting techniques. Don't listen to people like Star Sapphire and Cheetah. They don't know you."

"No one knows me," Barda said glumly. "I hear what they're saying about me. It's no big deal."

Batgirl and Supergirl watched her walk away again, neither knowing what to say.

"Trust absolutely no one," Katana warned as Batgirl kicked and punched the deadly aliens. They were all claws and teeth and made of hard rubber and steel. Katana pressed a button and a stun beam shot out of their eyes. Batgirl ducked. "Your opponent can never be underestimated," Katana continued. "You must always be on guard."

"What do you mean?" Batgirl asked.

"This!" Katana said, leaping up and bringing Batgirl down.

"Oof!" Batgirl cried. "Katana! Please remove your knee from my stomach!"

"Sorry!" Katana helped Batgirl up, then powered down the test aliens. She had to return them to the gym soon. Students were only allowed to check out robot adversaries in two-hour blocks. "I'm just saying that in battle, you have to be constantly aware. Never be complacent."

"You okay?" Supergirl asked, rushing toward them. She brushed some grass off Batgirl's costume. "Do you want to go to the school hospital? Do you need a bandage? Some water? A mint? Katana! Why did you do that?"

"I was just making a point," Katana said, flashing a no-nonsense smile. "She's fine. Batgirl's tough."

"I am fine!" Batgirl insisted. "Just not quite as indestructible as you, Supergirl."

A golden jar flew toward them. Batgirl could make out a tiny Bumblebee carrying it. Her friend grew to her full size. "For you!" she said, handing the jar over. "It's fresh honey—all-natural and delicious!"

Supergirl smiled. "Bumblebee knows the best places to get honey!" she said approvingly. "Be sure to eat this, Batgirl. And get enough rest. And exercise. Not just your mind, but your body as well, and . . . and . . ."

Batgirl knew Supergirl was just trying to be helpful—her fretful tendencies had come back full force as soon as Batgirl had agreed to be on TV. Supergirl was practically as overprotective as Batgirl's father, but at least she was more talkative.

". . . and don't worry," Supergirl was saying. "You'll do fine. Try not to freak out. Don't sit around thinking *Am I good enough? Am I smart enough? What if I mess up on live TV in front of millions of viewers? What if . . . ?"*

Batgirl gave her best friend a hug. It was one way to bring her back to reality. Because the truth was, Batgirl *was* freaking out.

As the Super Friends made their way to Capes & Cowls Café, they were all chatting and laughing and goofing off. Bumblebee was doing air ballet while Harley video-recorded her. Supergirl and Wonder Woman took to the sky to play hide-and-seek among the tall buildings, stopping midair to wave to the surprised office workers. Katana gracefully went through the motions of fighting imaginary ninjas. And weeds and flowers bloomed in Poison Ivy's wake. Everyone was having a great time, though Batgirl remained deep in thought—until she heard someone cry, "Save Rainbow!"

Before the last syllable was uttered, Batgirl shot her grappling gun. With the wire embedded into a thick branch, she easily hoisted herself up the tree. Within moments, she was cradling a calico cat in her arms.

"Rainbow is safe!" she assured the boy looking up from the ground.

The other Supers surrounded him, and he greeted them by name. "Hey, Wonder Woman! Hi, Supergirl! I like that flower in your hair, Poison Ivy. Katana, show me how to kick down a door!"

As Batgirl placed Rainbow in his arms, Harley looked into her video camera and reported, "Another super hero, another Rainbow rescue. It's almost a rite of passage that whenever there's a new Super in town, they have to rescue Rainbow!"

Harley zoomed in on the cat, which stared smugly at the camera and purred.

Batgirl thought she saw the cat wink. But no . . . impossible.

At the café, Steve Trevor was wiping down the tables. He froze when he saw Wonder Woman, and she did the same, causing Batgirl to bump into her and Supergirl to bump into Batgirl, squashing her between the two Supers.

"Batgirl, are you okay?" Supergirl said.

"I'm fine," Batgirl said, catching her breath.

"Well, *they're* not," Katana noted, pointing to Wonder Woman and Steve, who were still staring at each other in total silence, unaware that there were other people in the room.

"What?" Bumblebee asked. "What did I miss?"

Batgirl couldn't answer. Her thoughts were elsewhere. Her father was at the counter, holding a cinnamon doughnut in one hand and a tall cup of coffee in the other. But since she was still living at home, she thought it best to keep her normal identity on the down low. Here, she was Batgirl, not Barbara Gordon, daughter of Police Commissioner Gordon.

Commissioner Gordon smiled and waved at the heroes-in-training. He and Batgirl exchanged an additional nod, and then he walked out of the café, not even stopping to say hello.

CHAPTER 11

Later that night, Batgirl put the dishes in the dishwasher. She had souped it up and reconfigured it so that it took less than three minutes to wash and dry everything. With that done, she was settling down to do her homework when the doorbell rang.

"Barbara, I'm on an important call. Can you get that?" her father yelled from his study.

Batgirl opened the door. "Beast Boy!" she said. "What are you doing here?"

"This," he said, holding out a box.

"What's in it?" she asked, closing the door to her father's home office to give him privacy.

Beast Boy gently set down the blue shoe box. There were holes punched in the sides of the cardboard. "Someone left this outside the main entrance to the school. It has your name on it."

Gingerly, Batgirl lifted the lid.

"A baby bat!" she exclaimed. "It's so tiny!"

"It's injured," Beast Boy said, looking worried. "There was this, too." He handed her a sealed note, which she tore open.

"'Dear Batgirl,'" she read out loud. "'Please take care of this little one. She is an orphan and needs a good home.'"

"Who's it from?" Beast Boy asked, peering over her shoulder. He smelled like the root-beer candies he was always munching on.

"There's no name on it," Batgirl said, examining the paper. She folded it up and slipped it in her pocket, then turned back to the bat. It was hardly moving.

"Listen, I want to stay," Beast Boy said. "But I have to get back to school before Waller finds out I'm missing. There's no way I want to do detention again. Let's talk tomorrow, okay?"

Batgirl nodded, then rushed the box and the baby bat into her room. She didn't want to give her father something else to disapprove of.

Once she was alone, Batgirl looked at the bat. It was adorable, with its little wings and sweet face, its body no bigger than a strawberry. The soft blanket of gray-brown fuzz covering it made it look like a tiny stuffed animal. Batgirl logged on to her computer, then typed in *How to Care for Your Bat.*

Quickly, she fetched a soft face towel to line the box with. The bat was probably feeling vulnerable and would want something to snuggle in and hide under. Then she got a small bowl from the kitchen and filled it with water. But the bat wouldn't drink. Batgirl filled a straw with water, and with her thumb covering the top of it, she let go of one drop of water at a time into the bat's mouth.

Batgirl did this again and again as the bat drank eagerly. It was dark outside, but Batgirl drew the curtains in her room so that when the sun rose in the morning, the light wouldn't disturb the bat. Then she placed a hot-water bottle in the box to keep the baby warm.

While the bat slept, Batgirl built a comfy portable carrier for it. Since the baby bat would need constant care, Batgirl knew she needed to be close to it day and night. She tried different materials, settling on a heat-resistant plastic to regulate the bat's temperature. After lining the plastic with featherlight cushions, she fashioned a tiny water dispenser with a tube for sipping. Finally, she added a small camera inside so she could monitor the bat even when it was in her backpack.

Beast Boy was waiting for Batgirl when she got off the bus. "Is she okay?" he asked. Batgirl nodded. "What's her name?" The mischievous sparkle in his eyes complemented his green skin.

"I haven't decided yet," Batgirl said. She held her backpack close to her. The baby bat was nestled safely inside. Still, she was cautious. Batgirl was always cautious. She grabbed Beast Boy's arm, and they ducked into the school library.

"Can I help name her? Please, please?" Beast Boy begged. "I found her. I should be able to help. PLEASE!"

"Sure," Batgirl said.

"Please, please, please?" Beast Boy went on. "Puh-leeeeze!!!"

"Are you not listening?" she asked. "I said yes."

An impish grin lit up his face. "Well, all right, then!" He looked left and right before lowering his voice. "Batgirl, you do know there's a no-pets policy here at Super Hero High, right? That is, unless the pet in question has been approved by the PRC—the Pet Review Committee."

She nodded. She did know that. However, she also knew that the PRC took ages to approve a pet, and the bat needed a home now. Batgirl didn't want to do anything that would jeopardize her standing as a student at the school, but the baby needed her, and she had been brought up to believe that one should always help those in need.

"The bat isn't a pet." Batgirl was thinking out loud. By now they were in her Bat-Bunker. She dimmed the lights, and Beast Boy cradled the baby in the palm of his hand. "She's an orphan," Batgirl continued. "It's like I adopted her. She's family!"

Beast Boy perked up. "That's good. She's not a pet—she's a family member. So how about calling her Family Bat?"

"No," Batgirl said. Now it was her turn to hold the baby. It looked at her with its big eyes. "How about Baby Bat?"

"No," Beast Boy said. "How about Baby Batty?"

"I like that!" Batgirl exclaimed. "Or we could just call her Batty for short!"

The two friends grinned and gazed at Batty, who couldn't help looking adorable.

"You have a baby bat?" Supergirl asked. Her eyes widened. "Can I see?"

"No one can know," Beast Boy said as Batgirl lifted the lid of the carrier. Both looked around the library to make sure no one was watching them.

"It's adorable!" Supergirl squealed as the little creature took flight.

Batgirl blushed, proud as a mama bat. "Her name is Batty."

"Excuse me, but that isn't an unapproved pet, is it?"

The three turned to find Hawkgirl taking out her hall monitor detention-slip pad even though it was an hour before she went on duty.

"Bat? What bat?" Supergirl said. "Bat? There's no bat here. Rat, did you say rat? *Eek!* A rat!"

"You know there's a No Unapproved Pets rule here," Hawkgirl said, still looking around for a possible perpetrator.

"As hall monitor, I am going to have to report this."

"We're not in the hall," Batgirl pointed out.

Hawkgirl hesitated. "Yes, well . . ."

Just then, the baby bat flew in front of her, then around and around her, and then . . .

"Hi, Hawkgirl!"

Supergirl laughed and Batgirl tried to suppress a grin. This bat was green.

"Oh! H-hey, Beast Boy," Hawkgirl stammered as he smiled at her. "You're not a pet."

"Duh," Beast Boy said. He winked at Batgirl, who was frantically looking around the room for little Batty.

"Hey, Hawkgirl," Supergirl said, leading her out of the library. "Did you hear Red Tornado has assigned flights and flips in Flight class?"

Batgirl exhaled a sigh of relief. After a quick search, she found Batty sleeping peacefully near a pile of books. She was so small, it was hard to see her. "Thanks, Beast Boy," she said as the two gazed at Batty. "You were amazing."

"You are so right," he agreed.

"Hi, Dad," Batgirl called before rushing into her room. She took the small box from her backpack and opened it, cuddling Batty for a moment before setting her inside the darkened closet.

"Barbara," her father called back. "Come here, please."

Batgirl made sure Batty was safe and then ventured into the kitchen. Garlic and onions were sizzling in a pan. Her father was wearing a #1 Dad apron she had given him one Father's Day. Even though it was old and worn, he refused to get rid of it.

"Chicken à la Gordon and Gordon?" Batgirl asked.

He nodded. That was a joke between the two of them. Both loved his fried drumsticks, rolled in smashed Golden Goodie Flakes cereal, then fried up crispy and crunchy and seasoned with salt and pepper.

"Barbara," her father asked, turning up the heat. "Is there something you're hiding from me?"

Batgirl gulped. "What do you mean?" she asked.

How was it that her father always sensed when she was trying to get away with something? Batgirl knew for a fact that he wouldn't approve of Batty. When she'd wanted a dog, he said no. When she'd wanted a snake, he said no. When she was four years old and had wanted a tiger, he said no.

"I noticed that you've been somewhat secretive," he said as he gently laid the drumsticks in the skillet. They made a hissing sound when they hit the sizzling oil. "You aren't hiding something? I saw you and Beast Boy looking like you were up to something."

Batgirl watched the drumsticks turn a golden brown. She took a big breath. "Dad," she said. "There's something I need to tell you. . . ."

CHAPTER 12

Commissioner Gordon turned down the heat on the stove. He placed the chicken drumsticks on a paper towel to blot the oil. Then Batgirl transferred them to a platter, setting some aside for leftovers. (Cold fried chicken was a good midnight snack when studying late.)

"Well?" her father said as the two sat down for supper. He took a long drink of water. "What do you want to tell me, Barbara?"

Batgirl piled a scoop of mashed potatoes on her plate. "You asked me about the box?" she reminded him. "Well, I just wanted to tell you—there's nothing in it." That was true. There was nothing in it . . . at that very moment. Batgirl held her breath.

Commissioner Gordon's eyes narrowed. Batgirl knew he was an expert at interrogating criminals. But she wasn't a criminal. She was trying to save something.

"All right, then," her dad said, helping himself to the green beans. "I was just curious."

She exhaled.

"Was there anything else you wanted to say?"

Barbara wasn't sure what her father would think of the *TechTalkTV* invitation. He'd probably veto it, she thought. Commissioner Gordon always said that the only TV worth watching was the news.

"Well, I've been invited to be on a game show . . . well, not a game show, but a show about high tech, where the world's best compete," she said in a rush.

"Barbara!" her father said, setting down his fork.

"Yes?" she said hesitantly, holding her breath.

"That's great!" he exclaimed.

"It is?" she asked.

"Why, yes. This could lead to new opportunities for you. You could meet some techy contacts who can ultimately help you secure a job! Imagine that: Barbara Gordon, high-tech businesswoman. Has a nice ring to it, don't you think?"

Barbara looked away when she said, "Batgirl was invited, not Barbara."

"Oh," her father responded. She waited for him to say something else. "Barbara," he finally said, "do you think it's going to rain tomorrow?"

No one was happy with the Vehicle Training lesson that day. Least of all the teacher, Red Tornado. He would have preferred to have an extra Flight class, but Waller required that the Supers learn driving . . . within the speed limits and following the Metropolis City rules.

"That means *slooooooow,*" Red Tornado said, not even hiding his distaste.

"Why? Why do we have to do this?" asked The Flash as he did deep knee bends.

It was a rhetorical question. For the most part, the Supers were asked to test their limits. To go farther and faster than they ever had before. But now they had to adhere to the speed limit. What was with *that*?

"There may be times when you have to drive regular vehicles on regular roads," Red Tornado said. "If and when that's the case, you must abide by civilian rules. This is a safety issue." He looked at Supergirl, Katana, and The Flash. "This is also a test of your restraint. So for today, we will set aside your rocket ships, invisible vehicles, jet packs, and of course, your wings and powers of flight. Instead, we will be driving these."

There was an audible gasp as the door to the garage opened to reveal a fleet of old cars, trucks, vans, and motorcycles.

"Students, choose your vehicles!" Red Tornado shouted.

The initial complaints soon turned to laughter as the Supers tested out their vehicles. They drove too fast, veering off the road on purpose and bumping each other's vehicles, causing Red Tornado to dock points from everyone.

"Slow down!" he yelled as The Flash sped past him. "You are to use the motorcycle engine, not your legs, to propel your vehicle."

"Supergirl, put the car down and get into it and drive!"

"Cheetah, stop smashing into Miss Martian's electric car!"

"Wonder Woman, if the car in front of you isn't going fast enough, you DO NOT push it with your truck!"

Batgirl smiled as the wind blew in her face. She had never ridden a motorcycle before. It was almost like flying. As Red Tornado yelled at his students, Batgirl rounded the back roads, sticking to the speed limit and taking the curves with ease. She wondered what it would be like if she could soup up the engine and add a little Barbara-Assisted Technology to the motorcycle. Her smile grew wider as she pushed the engine harder.

Supergirl looked down at the B on her test, then at Batgirl's paper, then back at hers again. "I didn't know there was such a thing as an A+++. And why are they making fun of you?" she said, motioning to the garden bench where Cheetah and Star Sapphire were sitting.

"It's no biggie," Batgirl said, slightly disappointed that she didn't get an A++++. She made a mental note to ask her teacher if she could do more extra credit. "I got mocked all the time when I was at Gotham High, too."

Supergirl wrinkled her nose. "Really? 'Cause if it was me and people made fun of me, I'd be so stressed, I'd, I'd—" Her eyes lit up with the fire of her heat vision. "Well, I'd be a ball of stress."

Batgirl laughed knowingly and patted her friend on the back to calm her down. "Really, it's okay," she said. "There are worse things that could happen to me than people thinking I'm too smart!"

"Crisis negotiation is crucial in law enforcement!"

Though she was well aware of this, Batgirl took copious notes. Forensics, Law Enforcement, and You was one of her hardest classes—mostly because of the teacher.

"One must employ the following: active listening, empathy, rapport, and influence, all leading to behavioral change," Commissioner Gordon said, writing the points on the whiteboard. "Who can give me examples of these?"

Batgirl and Big Barda both raised their hands.

"Yes, Barda," he said, pointing to her.

"For example," Big Barda began, "say there was a villain

who was never given a chance to be good. If someone actually listened to her and grew to understand what she was really made of and a bond was formed, he could have a huge impact on her future as a super hero."

"Excellent! Excellent, Barda," Commissioner Gordon said proudly. "Class, you would do well to follow Barda's lead. This girl really knows what she's talking about!"

Big Barda glowed with happiness.

On the ride home from school, Batgirl turned down the police scanner. "Dad, may I ask you something?"

He didn't take his eyes off the road. "Sure, Barbara, what is it?"

She looked at the buildings rushing past them. "How come you never call on me in class? And how come you're so nice to Barda, but you seem to ignore me?"

Her father was silent for the next mile. "Barbara," he began, "Big Barda did not have the life you have. She's from Apokolips. Do you know what it's like there?"

Batgirl nodded. She had seen the videos in Liberty Belle's class. It was a desolate wasteland of war and the struggle for survival.

"This girl has had a hard life but is doing everything in her power to turn it around. Barda doesn't have a family, so

I'm doing what I can to make her feel welcome at Super Hero High and to make myself available whenever she needs to talk to someone. I hope you can understand that."

Batgirl felt a little guilty for being jealous of her friend, but she just couldn't help that she was.

"Sometimes I think you don't want me to succeed," Batgirl said flatly.

"What? *No,*" Commissioner Gordon said, sounding genuinely surprised.

"Yes, you do!" Batgirl didn't like what she heard herself saying, but she couldn't stop. "All the rules, putting me on probation . . . I want what Barda wants—to thrive at Super Hero High—but you aren't helping me at all. I totally understand that Barda needs to be accepted and supported, but, Dad, so do I. Instead of helping me, you're throwing roadblocks in my way!"

Commissioner Gordon pulled the car over to the side of the road. "I want you to succeed, Barbara," he said. "But I also want you safe. I want you to use your brains to find a place for yourself in this world. I want you to avoid all the bad stuff that fills so much of my life and the lives of the super heroes. I want so much for you, can't you see?"

Batgirl was seething, but she kept her cool. There was so much her father wanted for her. Yet he never listened to what she wanted for herself.

CHAPTER 13

The silence continued that night and through the week. Though they intersected in his class and during awkward dinners at home, it was as if Batgirl and her father lived separate lives. That made it easier to find excuses to study late on campus and sometimes crash with her bestie.

But over the next few weeks, her father seemed to recognize her need to study on campus and begrudgingly set her curfew back a few hours for late-night study sessions. And when she casually mentioned that it might be safer if she spent the night surrounded by the most powerful teens in the world rather than heading home so late, he started allowing her to stay the night.

"Thank you for letting me sleep in your room," Batgirl said to Supergirl one such night. She loved how cozy her BFF's room was, with the homemade quilt from her aunt Martha and the hand-carved Supergirl plaque from her uncle Jonathan.

"I like it when you're here," Supergirl told her as she raced around cleaning up, super-speed style. "I wish we could be roommates." She paused, then added, "I get lonely at night."

"I'd like that, too," Batgirl said. Batty was a terrific listener, but it was nice to have a two-way conversation.

With so much homework and so many tests, plus the *TechTalkTV* show looming, Batgirl was spending more and more time at school. She had started eating dinner in the dining hall, which led to attending group study sessions. Granted, they often turned into gab-fests with Bumblebee bringing honey crunch cookies and Poison Ivy offering everyone crisp apples from the school greenhouse. Inevitably, Harley would start cracking everyone up with her wacky *Would You Rather?* questions—a new segment on Harley's Quinntessentials.

"Would you rather fight an army of killer ants for an hour or walk around with five giant zits on your face for a week?" she asked, videoing everyone's response.

"Ants!" Wonder Woman said, smiling.

"Zits," Miss Martian said before disappearing.

"Ants!" said Big Barda.

"Zits!" Beast Boy said. "Ants are my friends."

"Ants, of course," Star Sapphire said, as if it were a dumb question.

Wonder Woman was a natural on camera. And so was Beast Boy. Bumblebee had a charismatic presence. Poison Ivy and Miss Martian made themselves scarce when the red video recording light was on. Batgirl wanted to avoid the camera, too—

"But you can't," Harley advised. "With *TechTalkTV* coming up, you need to be telegenic. The more the cameras love you, the better chance you have of winning."

"I thought the competition was all about my brain," Batgirl said. She had never seen Harley without her camera and wondered if she slept with it.

"Smarts, sweet tarts," Harley said, doing a backflip. "Yes, it's about how smart you are, but if the audience and judges don't like you, they won't vote for you. And if they don't vote for you, you don't win."

Is that true? Batgirl wondered.

"And in conclusion," Mr. Fox announced, "the upcoming Weaponomics student demonstration will commence in two weeks. I am expecting great things from all of you." He was looking directly at Batgirl.

Back in her Bat-Bunker, Batgirl set about creating new gadgets. The new and improved Batarang was coming along fine. Using the aerodynamic technology NASA employed, it worked like a boomerang, only better. Batgirl had the ability to loop around and change direction midflight, slice through cables and cars, and more. Still, her grappling equipment could use longer titanium wires, and she was experimenting with ones that were elasticized. Plus, her other tools and weapons, though impressive, could be even more so.

"Kick me harder!" Katana ordered Batgirl as she stood in the shade of the majestic maple tree. It had been just a sapling a day earlier, and then Poison Ivy worked her powers and botanical knowledge on it. Now it boasted leaves the size of pizza slices.

As Batgirl charged her at full speed, Katana yawned. "Don't be afraid to be strong," she reminded her. "Or to hurt or get hurt. It's all part of the plan."

Batgirl gritted her teeth and focused. As she sped toward Katana, gaining speed with each step, Batgirl leapt up and kicked hard. Katana brushed a bright orange leaf off her shoulder, then glanced up at the foot inches away from her head. She reached out with one hand, grabbed Batgirl's boot, and brought her friend crashing to the ground.

"You're getting better," Katana said, looking happy. Batgirl got up and nodded. When Katana did martial arts, she looked so graceful, like a ballerina—a really lethal ballerina. But when Batgirl tried the moves, she felt like a klutz. "Let's move on to weapons." Katana unsheathed the sword she always wore at her side.

Batgirl reached into her Utility Belt and whipped out a small metal cylinder.

"Is that it?" Katana asked, raising an eyebrow.

Batgirl smiled and pressed a button. The cylinder shot a yellow glowing ball into the air. It hit one of the clouds, leaving a large hole in it.

"That's more like it," Katana said approvingly as sunshine poured through the hole.

"You're doing great!" Supergirl exclaimed as they ducked and dodged the bullets, arrows, and other projectiles that hurtled their way. "Katana is a tough coach. For swords and hand-to-hand combat, she's the best."

Batgirl agreed but was too exhausted, mentally and physically, to respond.

"You're going to ace Fox's Weaponomics demonstration," Supergirl continued. "No one's better than you at creating new weapons. You're number one!"

Batgirl appreciated her best friend's enthusiasm but wished she would dial it down. It only put more pressure on her to succeed. And seriously, how could she, at this super-powered school? Being a super hero seemed to come naturally to almost everyone else. They were born with powers, or developed special skills at a young age. Her peers had been nurtured at super hero preschools, then super hero elementary and middle schools. Conversely, Batgirl was a latecomer and had to make up for a lot of lost time.

"It's not an issue," Bumblebee said. She was flying alongside Batgirl as the two participated in Team Clean, a new initiative Waller had instituted where Supers teamed up to pick up trash and talk, getting to know each other while doing something good for the school. Pairs of Supers roamed the school cleaning up as Parasite supervised. While some, like Supergirl and Poison Ivy, talked nonstop, other teams, like Hawkgirl and Catwoman, and Cyborg and Cheetah, didn't talk at all.

"I wasn't born with superpowers," Bumblebee was saying.

They crossed paths with Wonder Woman and The Flash, who were racing around seeing who could gather more garbage. "Slow down!" Wonder Woman cried. "You missed some trash!"

"No, *you* slow down," The Flash called back to her, laughing as she passed him up.

"You weren't born with powers?" Batgirl asked Bumblebee, surprised. "But you can fly! You can emit an electromagnetic sting-zap that can stop criminals and disable rockets."

"That's true," Bumblebee said, growing to her full size. "But those powers came to me just a few years ago, thanks to my bumblebee suit. I wasn't born with them."

"Do you ever feel that being born without powers holds you back?" Batgirl asked.

"Holds me back?" Bumblebee said. Her laugh was warm and light, like music. "It's the total opposite! Coming into powers late, attending Super Hero High, it's all a bonus.

Growing up a regular girl gives me insight into how the rest of the world lives. It's made me a better super hero."

Batgirl nodded. She hadn't thought of that.

"BREAK!" Waller called out. Everyone relaxed for the moment.

Big Barda was sitting on a bench alone. She lit up when Katana joined her and gave the former Fury an origami dragon she had just made.

As Batgirl approached, Barda held up the red paper dragon. "Look!" she said, holding it up as if it were a new jewel-encrusted Mega Rod.

"Barda, Katana," Batgirl asked. "What's your opinion about being a super hero?"

Cheetah strolled past and said, "Superpowers are not so much what you can do, but a state of mind. And my mind is made up. I was born to be a super hero . . . so I went out and got me some powers and abilities, and now I'm going to be a super being."

Barda didn't look as convinced. Before she had a chance to speak, Waller's voice blasted from the school's loudspeakers.

"SWITCH!"

There was a mad scramble as the Supers rushed to find a new partner. Batgirl noticed that Cheetah and Katana were now paired up. That wasn't going to go well.

Batgirl and Barda headed toward the vehicle garage. Adam Strange had crashed a rocket into Wonder Woman's Invisible Jet . . . which admittedly was difficult to see. And then, instead of cleaning up his mess, he fled the scene and ran right into Vice Principal Grodd. With Adam now sitting in detention, the remains of the crash were still there.

"Listen, Batgirl," Barda said as she carried the rocket to the DVL—Damaged Vehicle Lot—and set it down. "I have powers, and I still feel like I don't belong here. And I certainly don't feel like a super *hero*. People won't let me forget that I'm from Apokolips."

"You're going to be great," Batgirl assured her. "You know what it's like to train on enemy soil. But you have the heart of a super hero."

Barda pretended she had something in her eye and dabbed at it with a tissue. "I admire you, Batgirl," she said. "You're in this not for personal glory, but because you really want to help."

"I want to help, too!" Supergirl yelled as she flew overhead, surveying their work.

"Hi, Batgirl!" Cyborg yelled from the sky as he trailed Supergirl, using his rocket boosters. "Hi, Big Barda!"

Both waved to them.

"Thank you for believing in me, Barda," Batgirl said. She understood why her father had such faith in this former villain. "Let's agree to rise above our doubts and look forward, not backward."

"Agreed!" Big Barda said.

Batgirl raised her hand for a high five, and Barda hit her

so enthusiastically that she went hurtling fifty feet backward.

"Sorry!" Barda called.

"I'm not," Batgirl said as she rubbed her now-aching arm. "I'm glad we had this talk."

CHAPTER 14

There was no reason for Batgirl to be nervous. She had been looking forward to Mr. Fox's demonstration day. Still, this was her first big presentation at Super Hero High, and she wasn't sure what kind of response she'd get.

Cyborg went first. There was a large metal compactor in the front of the room, a scaled-down version of the kind used for crushing old cars. Without speaking, Cyborg got into it. He gave Mr. Fox a thumbs-up, and the teacher pressed a red button. Slowly, the massive compactor moved in on Cyborg, threatening to crush him. He raised his arms to his side as Batgirl held her breath. Cyborg closed his eyes tight and gritted his teeth as the machine made grinding noises and he fought against it, pushing metal against metal—finally bringing it to a halt.

Everyone applauded and Cyborg smiled. He had a nice smile. Cyborg lifted his arm to wave, and wave, and wave. It wasn't until a minute had passed that Batgirl realized he was malfunctioning and couldn't stop waving.

She rushed up to him and expertly adjusted his internal circuitry. His cybernetic arm often gave him problems when he was on overload. "You've just expended a lot of energy," she assured him. He shrugged sheepishly, as if to say that happens when you're half machine. "Listen, why don't you come to the Bat-Bunker later. I've got an idea for creating a feedback loop in your power coils that can override this kink in your circuitry."

"Thanks," Cyborg said, looking relieved. "That's a great idea."

Batgirl smiled. "That's what friends do for each other," she said.

"As long as you're already in the front of the room, why don't you go next, Batgirl?" Mr. Fox said. "What have you created for us to see?"

"Nothing," Batgirl said.

"Slacker," Frost whispered to Arrowette.

"N-nothing?" Mr. Fox stammered. He adjusted his glasses. "I don't understand. You knew today was demonstration day, correct?"

"Correct," Batgirl echoed. "But instead of bringing in some of the B.A.T. weapons I've developed, I thought I'd create some new ones on the spot. I plan to show the class how you can use ordinary objects to save the day."

Mr. Fox beamed. "Continue," he said, taking a seat.

"Who would like to give me something to begin with?"

Batgirl asked as she scanned the classroom.

Cheetah raised her hand. "Use this!" she said, flicking her wrist and tossing a pen to her. It cut through the air with the speed of a bullet, and Batgirl caught it with one hand.

"Thank you, Cheetah," she said, shifting the object to her other hand like a magician performing a trick and then throwing it back at her. But when Cheetah caught the pen, it released a plume of black smoke to surround her.

"I could have used more smoke powder," Batgirl explained. "But since this is merely a demonstration, I cut it down. Using the right amount could blur a villain's line of sight or just cause a distraction in a real battle."

Fox grinned, and Harley started recording.

Batgirl successfully set off everyone's phones as one big ear-shattering sonic disruptor, then turned a water bottle into a missile and transformed Mr. Fox's pocket watch into a detonator that exploded the water-bottle missile outside in the quad.

Even Cheetah had to admit with a purr and an arched eyebrow that Batgirl's ingenuity was pretty great.

"Which leads us to a subject I want to broach with all of you," Mr. Fox said when the cheers died down. "There was a time in the history of super heroes when one needed to have special powers—but that's not so anymore."

Cyborg looked at Batgirl. Everyone seemed to squirm in their seats for their own reasons.

"What," Mr. Fox asked, pausing for dramatic effect, "is the most powerful weapon in the world?"

"Kryptonite!"

"Sonic booms!"

"Swords!"

"An unbreakable lasso!"

"Power rings!"

"Brute force!"

Everyone had a guess.

Mr. Fox kept shaking his head. "Those are all good answers," he told the class. "But the most powerful weapon is one that all of you already have. Yet some of you are more capable of accessing it than others."

Everyone looked around.

"It's your brain!" the Weaponomics teacher shouted. "It's your brain and your ability to access it to its fullest! A keen mind can overcome any obstacle."

Big Barda nudged Batgirl and said, "You've totally got this covered!"

The commute was slowly killing her. Well, not literally, but it was a pain. Commissioner Gordon was on a huge case. So even when Batgirl was home in time for dinner, her father often was not.

"I know we can accommodate you," Principal Waller said, bringing up a layout of the dorms on her computer. "There's an empty room in Quad Seven."

Batgirl beamed.

"But," The Wall cautioned, "you must get your father's approval." Batgirl's shoulders slumped. "Good luck with that. Your father is one stubborn man. Brilliant, but stubborn."

Batgirl nodded knowingly.

"Take a seat," Waller ordered. "Let me tell you something about your father."

What could the principal tell her that she didn't already know? Batgirl wondered.

"Your father lets nothing stand in the way of justice," Principal Waller said. "There is no finer police officer in this country. When he first started, he was a maverick, taking all kinds of risks to catch the criminals and super-villains who sought to conquer and destroy Gotham City. But as he got older, he got smarter. He began taking fewer risks and making more concerted decisions. His dedication never wavered, but his approach to fighting crime did."

Her father used to be reckless? Never.

"Do you know *why* he is more methodical?" Waller asked.

Batgirl shook her head.

"Because of *you*," her principal said.

"Me?"

"You," Waller confirmed. "That man lives and breathes

for you. He knows that if anything happened to him, you'd be alone. And conversely, he would be devastated if anything happened to you. So he still takes risks, but they are calculated risks, and this has actually made him a better crime fighter. *You* have made him a better crime fighter.

"Batgirl," Principal Waller continued, "you have everything it takes to be a super hero—maybe even one of the greatest. But I sense that something is holding you back."

Batgirl blinked, not knowing what to say. Her father had changed his life . . . for her? But what he wouldn't do is change his mind and support her in her quest to be a super hero. Batgirl knew that the first step to making her dream come true was to fully immerse herself in Super Hero High. And that meant living at school. But how could she convince her father of that?

That evening Batgirl took the bus home to Gotham City. She rushed into her room to let Batty out of her carrier. The little bat had finally gotten strong enough to leave at home during the day.

Batgirl kept the lights off and shut the door to give Batty room to roam. Her father was still at work, so she started dinner.

"It smells good in here!" he said when he finally walked

through the door an hour later. As she passed the salad to him, Batgirl took note of his demeanor. He was in a rare good mood.

Her dad had taught her to read people's emotions. This wasn't a crisis negotiation, or was it? She remembered what he had taught the crisis negotiation class, and made sure to listen to what he had to say.

"It's a tough world out there," her father said as he speared a cherry tomato with his fork.

"It sure is, Dad," Batgirl said, nodding. "Just the other night when I was taking the Metro home, some shifty-looking characters boarded the bus."

He sat up. "Why didn't you call me? I would have come to get you."

"You were at work," she reminded him. "You work so hard, Dad," Batgirl noted, making sure to employ step two of the crisis negotiation: empathy.

"Well, yes, that can't be helped," her father said. "But I could have sent someone to get you. There's a lot going on right now. It's . . . well, there's a lot going on. Hey, it's supposed to be sunny tomorrow! How about that?"

"Sunny weather is great," Batgirl said, moving onto the rapport phase of the negotiation. "I love sunny weather. Only sometimes the weather can change so fast and it gets rainy at night."

"Yes, rain," her father agreed.

"Dad," Batgirl continued, gearing up for her compelling

argument. "I want to do well at school, and as you know, I have to stay late most nights." Her father nodded. "And with your work keeping you at the precinct and the Metro with its sketchy characters, well, I was thinking that if I got a motorcycle I could drive myself to and from school."

Batgirl waited for the color that had drained from her father's face to return a little before continuing. "In Vehicle Training, Red Tornado says I'm very skilled on the motorcycle, and I passed all the tests with flying colors. I even got my license! So what do you say, Dad? Motorcycle?"

He put down his fork, his face stern. "There is no way I'm going to let my daughter ride a motorcycle through the dark of night around Metropolis and Gotham City! It's not safe, not safe at all!"

"But, Dad," Batgirl insisted. "I have to stay late at school all the time, and I can't keep asking Supergirl if I can sleep on her floor. And you're too busy saving Gotham City to be my driver, and now the Metro is out of the question, so a motorcycle is our only answer."

Her father was silent. Batgirl could see him thinking. Finally, he said, "I would much rather you stay at school in the dorms than commute back and forth on a death machine on two wheels."

"*Stay at school?*" Batgirl said innocently. "I hadn't considered that. . . ."

"Yes, well," her dad said, thinking out loud. "Not every night. Just school nights. You would be here on weekends."

"Wow, do you think we could work it out?" Batgirl asked.

"I can make it work," he said, pushing his chair back and standing up. "I'm going to call Amanda Waller right now." As he was walking out of the room, he turned around and said, "A motorcycle? Seriously, Barbara, what were you thinking?"

She just shook her head. "I have no idea," Batgirl said, trying to suppress a smile.

CHAPTER 15

"She's here!"

Supergirl was carrying so many suitcases and boxes that all one could see of her were her red sneakers. Batgirl was ecstatic. At last, she was moving in to the Super Hero High School dorms!

"Let me help you with that!" Wondy said, taking some boxes and heading toward Batgirl's room.

Each dorm quad held four rooms that connected in the middle and had a shared bathroom. Batgirl's new roomies included Wonder Woman and Poison Ivy—who had put dozens of potted plants and flowers in her room as a welcome. And . . .

"The newest dormie at Super Hero High is Batgirl!" Harley Quinn announced to the camera. "Welcome, welcome to our quad. The best quad in the building. And boy, are we going to have fun!"

To prove this, Harley got out her mallet and used it like a

golf club, hitting all of Batgirl's boxes so that they flew in the air and piled up on top of each other.

"Ahem. Barbara, may I have a word with you in private?" a voice said from the doorway.

Batgirl had been so excited she'd forgotten her father was there.

"What is it, Dad?" Batgirl asked as Poison Ivy and Wonder Woman excused themselves.

Commissioner Gordon cleared his throat and looked at Harley. She shrugged. "Okay, okay, I get it, Commish. You want me out of here, too, right?"

"Yes, thank you, Harley," he said, picking up her camera from the desk. The red record light was on. He thumbed it off. "Oh, and you left this."

"Oops! My bad," Harley said sheepishly as she grabbed the camera and cartwheeled out of the room.

Batgirl noticed that her father had some more gray hairs. When did he get those?

"I know what you're going to say," Batgirl said, eager to start unpacking and get settled. "And I want you to know that I'm going to be just fine here. Actually, more than fine. All my friends are here, and Principal Waller and the other teachers will look after me. The food in the dining hall isn't as good as your cooking, but it's not half bad, and I won't starve. I'm not a little girl anymore. This is going to be really good for me. I'll keep up my grades, I promise. If anything, they'll get even better!"

She stopped when she noticed that her father looked like he was going to cry.

"Dad?"

He started to speak, but nothing came out. Batgirl felt a lump in her throat. How could she be so blind? she wondered. It wasn't that her father was worried she was going to have a hard time adjusting to living away from home. No, it was her dad who would have the hard time.

Batgirl gave him a big hug. "It's going to be okay, Dad," she assured him. "You're going to be okay. We'll see each other twice a week in class. Plus, we can talk on the phone or even AboutFace on the computer. Or if you want, we can go totally old-school and write letters to each other. And I'll be home on weekends . . . unless there's a big project."

Commissioner Gordon looked lovingly at his daughter. "Babs," he said, trying to smile but not doing a very good job of it. "When did you get to be so tall? And so mature? It seems like it was just yesterday you were learning to walk, and now this." He motioned to her boxes and suitcases.

"It'll all work out, Dad," Batgirl said. "You just call if you need me and I'll be right there for you."

"Okay, Barbara." He straightened up and took a deep breath, then added, "Now, don't do anything that could put you in danger!"

"Yes, Dad."

"And don't go outside without a sweater if it's cold!"

"Yes, Dad," Batgirl said again and again until he ran out

of things to be worried about. Then she hugged him one more time and sent him on his way. *Parents,* Batgirl thought fondly. *They need so much care and attention.*

That night the dining hall was bustling. Students were carrying trays, levitating them, and teleporting their dinners across the room. Supergirl had used her heat vision to charbroil her undercooked hamburger, while Catwoman was being accused of taking the last piece of cake, which was being saved for someone else.

"How do you deal with it?" Batgirl asked.

"My parents write to me all the time, telling me to be careful, that swords are sharp," Katana volunteered. "I assure them that I'm a stickler for safety."

"My parents expect me to check in with them every other day," Bumblebee said. "So I put it on my calendar, because one time I forgot and they were certain that I was in mortal danger, when really, I was cooking up a new kind of honey-crunch vitamin cereal bar . . . though King Shark *had* tried to swallow me earlier that day."

"I wish my parents were here to worry about me," Supergirl said.

"I'll worry about you!" Batgirl said reassuringly.

"I will, too," Katana joined in.

"We'll all take care of each other!" Bumblebee added.

Batgirl smiled. She was starting to feel at home.

It didn't take long to unpack. With Supergirl's super-speed, Wonder Woman's organizational skills, and Katana's sense of style and substance, her room looked like it had been there from day one of school. It had blue and purple walls, plenty of shelf and desk space, a ladder leading up to her loft bed, and all kinds of secret compartments. Still, it felt incomplete to Batgirl, but she'd need Principal Waller's permission to do what she wanted to do.

"That's a great idea," The Wall said the next day, to her relief. "I'm interviewing new IT people to replace you, and they'll want to use the annex. Now that you're living here, yes, you can move all your computers and equipment into your room and it can be the new Bat-Bunker! Of course, you'll have to enhance the dorm security."

"I've already drawn up the plans!" Batgirl assured her.

"WARNING! WARNING! WARNING!"

"Wowza, that's loud!" Harley cried, covering her ears. "And wouldn't just one 'warning' do?"

"There's a lot of expensive high-tech equipment in here," Batgirl explained. "I have to make sure it's safe. In the wrong hands, it could be dangerous."

Harley picked up a small metal box and started shaking it.

"Please don't do that," Batgirl said. She was relieved that Batty was safely sleeping in her closet. "That's a long-range mini-detonator I'm developing. It can detect, assess, and access any explosive within a ten-mile radius."

"Whoa!" Harley set it down and backed away. "You sure have lots of keyboards," she said as she pretended to be playing the piano.

Batgirl took the keyboard away from her.

"What's this?" Harley asked, picking up a metal wire that was bent in a peculiar shape.

"A paper clip," Batgirl said. She reminded herself to add even more locks and security to her new Bat-Bunker.

CHAPTER 16

"**W**ould you mind taking on a temporary assignment?"

Batgirl pivoted. She was shelving books in the library. Even though she loved all things high-tech, there was something comforting about an old-fashioned book. The way it smelled. The turning of its pages. The heft of it. The *information.* She enjoyed being a library volunteer. Her father had always said that being a librarian was a noble job, and that perhaps it was a vocation she should consider. Her mother had been a librarian.

"I've hired a new tech whiz to replace you," Waller explained as though Batgirl had already agreed. "But she can't start for a while."

Batgirl nodded. Even though she was no longer the school's official tech whiz, students hadn't stopped asking for her help.

"Maybe your first temporary assignment can be a fingerprint lock for my jewelry safe," Star Sapphire said.

She was wearing matching diamond earrings and a necklace. Everything down to the jeweled buttons matched. Batgirl thought about what it all must have cost and the kind of equipment she could have bought with that money.

"Sure thing," Batgirl said. "I can have that installed in two days."

"Make it one," Star Sapphire said, walking away.

"You do know where her family gets their money, don't you?" Batgirl looked at the fuzzy bear standing next to her. He was eating a pumpernickel sandwich. She never knew what animal Beast Boy would be.

"Sapphire's father is an aerodynamics mogul who owns and operates Ferris Aircraft," Batgirl replied. It was common knowledge.

"So you do know? I was just testing you," Beast Boy said. "Is there anything you *don't* know?"

Batgirl dimmed the lights as Batty flew around the room. Only Beast Boy and Supergirl knew about her little bat. Beast Boy turned into an identical bat, and as he played with Batty, Batgirl thought about Star Sapphire's family fortune. It would be nice to be as rich as that. Although . . . if she won *TechTalkTV,* she'd have the prize money—and with that, she could give her B.A.T. tech a major upgrade.

Katana waved to Steve Trevor. "May we please have two more orders of sweet potato fries?" she called above the chatter in the café.

Poison Ivy smiled and the tulips on the flower box outside the window suddenly began to bloom.

As Steve headed toward them with two tall plates of sweet potato fries, Ratcatcher from CAD Academy threw a trap in front of him. Before it even landed, Wonder Woman used her Lasso of Truth to whip it out of the way.

"He says he doesn't have powers," Wonder Woman noted as she watched Steve walk away. "But whenever I'm around him, I feel funny inside and can't talk!"

"It's just a crush," Katana said as she munched on the fries.

"From what I understand about crushes," Wonder Woman said earnestly, "you're not supposed to really crush the person who likes you, or vice versa. Also, don't throw a plate at someone's head. They don't like that."

Katana rolled her eyes good-naturedly at Batgirl and explained, "When Wonder Woman first came from Paradise Island, she thought a plate was a Frisbee and knocked Steve out."

Batgirl tried to suppress a laugh. Though Wonder Woman

was one of the most famous super hero teens in the world, and a great strategist and leader when it came to fighting evil, she still could be pretty naive.

"I don't know," Poison Ivy said as the tulips kept changing colors. "I'm not sure I'd know what to look for in that special person. It's almost as if I need a cheat sheet!"

"That's a great idea," Supergirl said, pulling up a new notes page on her phone. "Let's each make a list of the top three attributes our dream person should have."

- Supergirl: courage, strength, kindness
- Poison Ivy: compassion, motivation, loyalty
- Wonder Woman: strength of character, compassion, Steve
- Hawkgirl: stability, strength, honesty
- Batgirl: intelligence, strong sense of justice, sense of adventure
- Harley: sense of humor, daring, unpredictability
- Katana: creativity, sharp wit, honor

Back in the Bat-Bunker, Batgirl immediately went to check on Batty. The little bat was strong as she flew around the room, playfully buzzing Batgirl before alighting on her shoulder.

"Ah, Batty. It's so great to have someone to talk to," Batgirl said as she logged on to several of her computers, checking on her temporary-tech-whiz to-do list. Star Sapphire's name was on it several times. "Boys are terrific, but boys are a distraction, and right now I need to focus on school and the *TechTalkTV* show."

CHAPTER 17

Cyborg's systems were bothering him, though he tried to be stoic. He had a pounding headache so loud that Beast Boy could actually hear it. Cyborg's green friend said, "Seriously? Chill, Cyborg, this isn't drama class!"

"Are you okay?" Batgirl asked as Cyborg closed his eyes and held his head with both hands.

"I'm fine," he said. The look of pain was evident.

"Let me make sure." Batgirl reached for her Utility Belt.

She ran a full robotics check, but she could find nothing wrong. "I don't know what happened," she said. "You seem to be in perfect working order."

"I'm thinking of upgrading my operating system," Cyborg said, "but it's such an extensive project, and, well . . ."

Batgirl nodded. There were a lot of things that could go wrong during an upgrade. "You know I'll have your back," she assured her friend.

He smiled. "It's not my back I'm worried about."

Batgirl nodded again. Those were tricky things. "We'll run a full analysis on you," she promised. "We techies have to take care of each other."

Batgirl's schedule was full from the moment she woke up to the moment she went to sleep. Plus, she'd wake up in the middle of the night, worried that she was forgetting something—or worse, she'd remember something that she had in fact forgotten to do.

"Are you nervous?" Supergirl asked on the way to class. "Beause if I were you, I'd be really, really, really nervous."

Batgirl shook her head. "I'm okay," she said, sounding unconvinced.

"It's okay to be nervous," Supergirl said as Batgirl rappelled to the top of the Amethyst Tower.

"Millions of people will be tuning in live to watch the competition, but that doesn't faze you?" Supergirl asked. They were now at the top of the tower. Supergirl removed the heavy crystal so Batgirl could examine the electronics that monitored the school icon.

"Nope," Batgirl said. She spotted an outdated gem-fi connector at the base of the pedestal and replaced it. Supergirl put the Amethyst back in place and all hummed back to life. Sometimes something simple could cause the most chaos.

"You're not scared that when they ask you the hardest tech questions in the world, you'll forget the answers?" Supergirl asked, depositing the crystal back on its stand.

"Nope," Batgirl said. She opened her new retractable Batwings and glided to the ground. Creating them had cost more than she had budgeted.

"You're not nervous that your dad will be watching and that you'll mess up and he'll want to pull you out of Super Hero High?" Supergirl asked, landing alongside her.

"Huh? Oh! Oof! Ouch!" Batgirl said, getting up and brushing herself off. Okay, *now* she was nervous.

Even when she was very young, Batgirl relished taking tests. Oh, sure, studying was fun, but the tests themselves were when the real excitement started.

With the TV show scheduled for the next day, Batgirl sealed off the Bat-Bunker for maximum privacy. Harley Quinn had a habit of barging in at the most inopportune times. "Can you say a few words for Harley's Quinntessentials?" she was always asking, putting her camera in Batgirl's face.

As Batty flew around the room, Batgirl called up her spreadsheets on the computer. There were photos of the other competitors, plus bios of each. She studied them carefully. "Always know who and what you're up against," her father had taught her.

The competition would be fierce. She was facing:

- Master Miser, a genius whose lifelong passion was to bring cheap computers to the world
- Dr. Eloise Lee, founder of multimillion-dollar multinational cutting-edge computer companies
- Noah Kuttler, the teenager with the highest recorded CompuQ score in the world
- Almighty Dolores Dollar, creator of a new currency system based on computer chips
- Alpha Numeric, an infamous code breaker who was rarely seen in public

Batgirl reviewed her notes. She was grateful that her friends had been so helpful. Harley had done well with her media training, teaching her how to speak up and look into the camera.

Katana had taught Batgirl to slow down and get in touch with her inner self—to not just react, but to act accordingly and listen to her instinct.

Bumblebee had told her to enjoy her moment in the spotlight, not fear it.

Poison Ivy had reminded her that even though she might not like being in the spotlight, she was representing all of Super Hero High.

Wonder Woman had worked with Batgirl on her physical

strength, telling her it was important to be healthy and strong, inside and out.

Hawkgirl instructed her to listen to the rules and what was being said, and not to jump to conclusions.

Big Barda had said, "Power up, then knock 'em down!" as she jabbed at an imaginary contestant.

And Supergirl had hugged her tight and assured her, "You're going to do great, Batgirl, I just know it. If anyone can conquer a high-tech contest, it's you!"

Batgirl thought about the one person who had not given her any advice, the person she most longed to hear from: her dad. Though it was after midnight, she began writing an email. Would he be in the audience? she wondered. Would he even watch?

The whole school and beyond was tuning in. Lois Lane, who had her own must-read news blog, had interviewed Batgirl just the other day. And Harley was doing daily reports about the competition.

It seemed like everyone, even strangers, were wishing her good luck. But in class, Commissioner Gordon didn't even acknowledge Batgirl. However, she did notice that he always praised Barda when she got an answer correct.

Dad, I hope I'll see you . . . , Batgirl typed.

She hit delete. If he wanted to be there, he would.

Batty had been asleep for hours when Batgirl slipped under her covers. On her nightstand was a framed photo. She picked it up and stared at it. It showed a little girl sitting on the strong shoulders of her father. Both were grinning wildly.

"Good night, Dad," Batgirl said to the photo. "I want you to be proud of who I am."

Batgirl felt warm when she heard him say, "Good night, my Babs. I am proud of you."

Then she realized it was just her imagination.

CHAPTER 18

Supergirl examined the table. Assorted fresh fruits and colorful candies, and crunchy crackers and smelly cheese, competed for space. Cookies decorated with the faces of the competitors graced a silver tray. She reached for a water bottle. "Why do they call it the greenroom when the walls are white?" Supergirl asked.

Batgirl shook her head. "It's just what they call a waiting room for TV shows and things like that."

"Are you nervous?" Supergirl said through a mouthful of grapes.

"I'm okay." Batgirl suppressed a yawn. She hadn't slept well. She wondered if her father was in the audience.

"Here, eat this!" Supergirl handed her a cookie.

Batgirl stared at her own face on the cookie. There was too much frosting on her nose, making it look unusually large or like she had a pimple.

A young woman wearing a *TechTalkTV* shirt and a headset

yelled, "Get ready to go on in five minutes." She held up her fist and then opened her hand and waved her fingers in the air. "Five!"

"Got it!" Batgirl assured her.

Alicia Chen strolled into the room. Supergirl gaped at her chic red outfit and sky-high heels. Sparkles spewed from a tiny hat perched on her head. "Batgirl! So happy to have you on board," Alicia gushed. "Just wanted to wish you luck." She embraced Supergirl. "Big fan, big fan of yours, Supergirl. I'm thinking of producing a teen super hero reality series. Here." She handed her a business card and left.

Supergirl stared at the photo of Alicia Chen on her card. And then it winked at her.

The woman with the headset showed up again. "Two minutes!" she called out. She brushed the sparkles left in Alicia's wake off her shirt.

"Okay, I gotta go. Wonder Woman is saving my seat," Supergirl said, rushing out. She returned in a split second and gave Batgirl a huge hug. "I'm rooting for you. We all are!"

The audience was packed with students from Super Hero High. Principal Waller and all the teachers were there, too. Well, all but one. Where was he?

"Batgirl!" someone shouted. She looked at Doc Magnus, who held up a handmade Go, Batgirl! banner.

She smiled and waved to him. Maybe her father was just late? He wouldn't want to miss this, would he? Just then, she got a message on her computer watch.

"What is it, Cyborg?" she asked.

"Your dad," he said. Was he okay? Batgirl wondered. "Lois Lane intercepted an anonymous tip that Killer Croc and Solomon Grundy are robbing the Metropolis Movie Theater this afternoon. Your father plans to be there to greet them."

Batgirl thanked Cyborg and tried not to look disappointed. She had really wanted her father there. But as she looked around, she was heartened that her friends were present to cheer her on.

"BOOM!" Big Barda yelled, once again punching an imaginary opponent.

"Go, Batgirl!" Cyborg called out. He had *Team Batgirl* written across his forehead.

As the other contestants were led onstage, Batgirl looked them over. She was already familiar with each one, having done her research. The lights dimmed and the studio audience hushed as a soothing voice announced from above, "Welcome to *TechTalkTV*'s high-tech competition, featuring the brightest techno brains in the world! And now . . . let's hear it for the *TechTalkTV* impresario and your host for the evening, the brilliant blogger and tech expert extraordinaire, Nebble Bytes!"

Batgirl felt giddy when a slight man with a nebbish look on his egg-shaped face wandered onto the stage, getting lost at one point. The woman with the headset led him to the podium. Batgirl had been a fan of Nebble Bytes ever since she was a little girl. To be on the same stage with him was an honor.

One by one, Nebble Bytes introduced the contestants. Batgirl could hardly believe the kind words he had for her, calling her one of the smartest, most talented teens around. Unaccustomed to such public accolades, she couldn't help blushing. As she did, Batgirl noticed that Noah Kuttler, the other teen competitor, held a toothy smile while she was being introduced.

Then Nebble Bytes invited each one to his podium. "Your platform," he said, looking serious. "Tell us, what does tech mean to you?"

Master Miser: "Computers for everyone!"

Dr. Eloise Lee: "The tools to run the world from a desk!"

Noah Kuttler: "Bringing understanding and respect to the tech industry!"

Almighty Dolores Dollar: "A world economy based online!"

Alpha Numeric: "International and interplanetary exchange of information!"

Batgirl blinked against the bright lights again and looked out into the audience. Harley was giving her signals to stand up straight, smile, and enunciate.

"To make the world safer and smarter via tech!" Batgirl said, her voice strong and confident.

As the audience roared their approval, Nebble Bytes introduced the celebrity judges—a high-tech titan, a socialite turned chef, an Academy Award–winning actress who played a computer whiz, and a basketball player who had written a children's book. More cheering ensued, helped out by a state-of-the-art studio system that amplified sound fivefold. Next, it was time for the rules. Batgirl listened carefully.

"The preliminary round goes by simple numbers—who gets the most right," Nebble explained quickly. "For round two, it's by the numbers and judges' selections. In the final round, where the big tech test comes in, it comes down to the master computer's tally of audience picks, judges' picks, Internet audience favorites, and the numbers."

The audience looked confused, but the contestants appeared confident. "Let's kick this off with a lightning round," he said, grinning into the camera and trying to wink. "Watch out!"

Batgirl and her fellow contestants jumped back as glass podiums with metal buzzers rose from the floor in front of them. The audience applauded as the cameras panned the seats, getting close-ups of many of the Supers, including Beast Boy, who made a funny face, and Star Sapphire, who clapped politely but did not seem to be showing interest.

Nebble began. The questions were so complex the audience let out a series of oohs and aahs, even though, or maybe because, they didn't understand them. It was a close round, but in the end, Batgirl won by a small margin, with a huffy Alpha Numeric coming in half a point behind her.

The show moved quickly, and Batgirl was surprised by how much she was enjoying it. The training from her friends helped.

"The second competition pairs up the top tech heads to create a new computer program—one the world has never seen before," Nebble Bytes announced gleefully.

Batgirl looked around, wondering who her partner would be. She hoped it would be Dr. Eloise Lee, who was credited with the downsizing of the desktop computer and its accessories. Dr. Lee nodded to her.

Noah Kuttler, the other teenager, was watching Batgirl. His highwater pants revealed mismatched socks, and he wore a funny T-shirt about HTML code. An impressive mass of unruly brown hair sat atop his head.

"Dr. Eloise Lee and Alpha Numeric!" Nebble Bytes called out as the two linked hands and raised them in the air like champions.

Batgirl braced herself. Who would her partn—

"Noah Kuttler and Batgirl!" Nebble Bytes announced as their photos appeared on a huge screen behind them. "The tech teens!"

Embarrassed, the two smiled at each other. It could have been worse, Batgirl noted. In her research she had learned that Almighty Delores Dollar was stingy with her money and was known for having a sour disposition, and that Master Miser, though jolly, was famous for throwing hissy fits. Noah seemed like a good match.

As the celebrity judges were given the stage to talk about their latest projects, the duos were led into glass booths where their discussions could not be heard. Inside each was a table with two state-of-the-art computers; limitless CoffeeCoffee, a new brand and sponsor; and a timer set to fifteen minutes. Fifteen minutes. That wasn't much time to create a new computer program.

"It's because this is TV time," Noah said as he logged on.

Batgirl did the same. Teamwork would be important here. "I was thinking that we could create a new anti-deprogramming program," she suggested. "One to get the bugs out of new programs that haven't been fully vetted yet."

Noah ran his hand through his hair and tugged at it. "That's a good idea," he said. He took a big gulp of coffee. "But I've been toying with a holographic equation that could change the way we assess our deliverables."

Batgirl took in a sharp breath. She had been thinking about this very same thing just last week. "Yes! One day we can turn the Internet into a true and literal transportation highway. Let's do it!" she said eagerly. "Holograms as placeholders today but as true transporters tomorrow!"

Never one to hog the credit, Batgirl was excited to learn more from Noah. Perhaps, she suggested as they cranked out code, they could keep in touch after the show.

The timer was counting down. They had less than a minute left. Then—

"Time's up!" Nebble Bytes cried as the computers shut down in unison.

Batgirl could see but not hear Master Miser and Almighty Delores Dollar yelling at each other. Dr. Eloise Lee and Alpha Numeric looked smug. She turned to Noah, who appeared to be spacing out, looking blankly into the audience.

"Noah," she said, giving him a nudge. "We're ready to go."

It was a close call. The celebrity judges deducted major points from Master Miser and Almighty Delores Dollar for not finishing within the allotted time. Dr. Eloise Lee and Alpha Numeric had created a simple but ingenious code to assist in the streamlining of credit applications that had the judges nodding, though clearly not understanding.

Last up were Batgirl and Noah Kuttler.

"Tech teens!" Nebble Bytes shouted. "We can't wait to see what the future of tomorrow will show us today!"

Noah cleared his throat nervously. He and Batgirl had decided that he would be the one to speak. But when he looked into the camera, he only got out a few mumbles and then froze, so Batgirl stepped forward. Employing her interviewing skills, Batgirl demonstrated the Hologram XLABCXYZ Equation. It was so complex that the audience sat stunned. "And with this," she concluded, "it's just a matter of time before we can send fully rendered holographic 3-D images from computer to computer."

Noah suddenly got over his bout of stage fright and grabbed the microphone from her. "That's right," he said triumphantly, but by then the judges were conferring and typing furiously into their computers. The time was up.

After a commercial break, Nebble Bytes was handed an electronic envelope. "If only I were a mind reader," he quipped as he held it to his forehead. The audience laughed. Then he pressed a button and the envelope unfolded, revealing the decision. "The winners of the Tech Team round are . . ."

CHAPTER 19

"The tech teens have won the all-important second round!"
Nebble Bytes announced, looking pleased.

Batgirl and Noah Kuttler jumped up and down as they
congratulated each other. Their competition looked like they
had just sucked on lemons. The Super Hero High contingency
in the audience roared their appreciation, and several of the
Supers were asked by security to power down as they flew
and bounced around the studio.

During the next commercial break, Batgirl said to Noah,
"Good luck in the final round."

"My parents don't think tech is a big deal," Noah admitted.
He was eating cookies with both hands. "My dad's an organic
carrot farmer, and my mom raises llamas and weaves caps
from their wool. They don't even own a computer."

Batgirl understood. Though her father had a turbocharged
computer, thanks to Batgirl, it was clear that *TechTalkTV*
wasn't a big deal to him. If it were, he'd be there, right?

Both Noah and Batgirl were silent for a moment.

A familiar voice from above announced, "We're back on the air live in one minute. Places, everyone!"

There was complete silence in the studio, except for a nervous *ping* coming from inside Cyborg. The celebrity judges sat stone-faced. Nebble Bytes raised his hand in the air. "The final round is a computer conundrum," he said. "That's right! Our competitors must break a complex code virus, upload it onto their computers, and neutralize it, under stressful conditions. Not only will they be timed and scored for accuracy, but the celebrity judges will also cast their votes. Wait! And there's more, because we're asking our studio and television audiences to weigh in as well!"

The audience cheered wildly, until Nebble Bytes demanded, "SILENCE, PLEASE!"

When the audience wouldn't stop cheering, Cyborg let out a sonic blast from his cybernetic arm that instantly quieted the room. Alicia Chen took his name and handed Cyborg her card as Nebble Bytes nodded his appreciation.

The contestants were serious as they approached a state-of-the-art computer station. This was their big chance to win. Cameras recorded from every angle. As a confusion of letters, numbers, and symbols scrolled onto each computer screen, the audience gasped. The code was so dense it looked like a block of black. Batgirl and the others leaned forward and squinted to get a better look.

This is going to be tough, Batgirl thought. She glanced at Noah, who was hunched over, typing furiously, his brow knotted and his teeth clenched. Suddenly, there was the squall of a baby crying. Then the menace of a dog barking, then the smash of vehicles crashing. That was just the first wave of distractions.

The temperature in the studio plummeted to freezing cold, and suddenly the Wi-Fi connection started going in and out as a team of mimes entered with chalkboards and ran their fingernails down them.

"We are simulating less-than-ideal conditions," Nebble Bytes said gleefully as the distraction ramped up to epic proportions.

Finally, one of the competitors yelled, "I GOT IT! I FIGURED IT OUT!"

Batgirl looked at Noah Kuttler as he did an awkward victory dance back and forth across the stage, all traces of his stage fright gone. Almighty Delores Dollar frowned, and Alpha Numeric shook his head. The audience slowly went silent as Noah continued to dance.

Nebble Bytes took to the podium and broke the silence. "Noah Kuttler has solved the computer conundrum!" he announced. "He has broken apart the complex code and boiled it down to its essence. Therefore, he takes the third and final round."

"I'm number one!" Noah cried, breaking into an awkward moonwalk and then spiking his calculator so that it shattered, sending parts flying into the first row and hitting some audience members. "Noah Kuttler is in da room!"

Nebble Bytes cleared his throat and tried to get the attention of some of the disgruntled audience members. "And now it is time for you, celebrity judges"—he motioned to them—"to cast your vote for the *TechTalkTV* champion. And for you, TV audience"—he motioned to the camera and winked—"to cast your vote for the *TechTalkTV* champion. And for you, studio audience"—he motioned to them—"to record your pick on the panel in front of you and help select the *TechTalkTV* champion."

Supergirl hit the Batgirl button so hard she destroyed it and had to ask for a new one.

Nebble Bytes continued. "TV viewers, we are counting on you to log in or call and vote for your favorite *TechTalkTV* competitor! A team of accountants and I will also tabulate the scores and, using an algorithm too advanced for you to ever understand, we will crown the *TechTalkTV* champion and winner of the mega money. But first, this important message from our sponsor, CoffeeCoffee, with twice the caffeine for half the price!"

Backstage, the adults were reluctantly congratulating Noah Kuttler. All signs pointed to him as the champion.

He and Batgirl had won the team competition, and he had won the final round. Still, the celebrity judges, audience, and viewer votes had to be tabulated.

"You were a great teammate," Noah said to Batgirl.

"I can learn so much from you," she told him. "Congratulations!"

He blushed. "I hope my little dance didn't cost me too many points," he said, looking sheepish. "But you're right, I've got this in the bag. If my parents are even watching, maybe they'll finally take notice of what I'm capable of."

Batgirl wondered if her father was watching—he was on a big case that seemed to be keeping him busy. Even though she was sure she didn't win, Batgirl knew she had done her best.

The competitors stood onstage. Nebble Bytes held up a sealed envelope as a spotlight shone on it. Noah Kuttler tried not to look too happy, but it was difficult for him. The adults looked like they had eaten slugs. Batgirl was happy the competition was over and she could get back to school.

"And the winner is . . . ," Nebble Bytes said, opening the envelope, then leaning into the microphone, "BATGIRL!"

As confetti fell from the rafters, the audience went crazy. Batgirl could hear Supergirl cheering louder than the rest, which was no mean feat, considering how loud Cyborg and

Harley were. Even Principal Waller got in a "Woot woot!" before she composed herself. Doc Magnus looked so proud that Batgirl thought he might burst. Batgirl herself stood frozen, not knowing how to react.

Master Miser threw a hissy fit, storming off the stage. Dr. Eloise Lee congratulated Batgirl, but her handshake was weak and insincere. Alpha Numeric looked directly at her and said, "You won—this time." And Almighty Delores Dollar turned her back on Batgirl.

"Noah?" Batgirl said as they were led offstage. She was carrying a giant check for $25,000. "Are you okay?"

"Of course I'm not okay. YOU JUST STOLE MY WIN!" he yelled, his eyes flashing. He looked scary but instantly calmed down before slumping over. "I'm sorry, Batgirl," he said then. "It's just that I thought I had done well. I thought I was going to win."

"You did! More than good, you were amazing," she consoled him. "It should have been you holding this." She handed him the golden circuitry-board trophy she'd been given in addition to the prize money.

Noah held it gently, then reluctantly passed it back to Batgirl. "It's yours," he said. "The people have spoken. They liked you more than me. Story of my life. The end."

CHAPTER 20

Batgirl was unsettled. Luckily, she had Batty to confide in. "All the interviews, all the attention, all the everything," she told the little bat. "It's overwhelming."

Batty flew around the Bat-Bunker, then hung upside down on the lamp on the corner of Batgirl's desk. If only life were as calm everywhere as it was in the Bat-Bunker, Batgirl thought. She loved being alone with her tech. Just that afternoon at Capes & Cowls Café, Captain Cold had frozen Batgirl's chair right before she sat down, causing her to slide off and fall on the floor.

"Now, is that a way for a champion to behave?" he asked as Batgirl picked herself up.

"Leave her alone!" Katana demanded, instantly at her side. She only had to put her hand on the hilt of her sword to make Captain Cold and his CAD Academy cohorts, Ratcatcher and Magpie, back away.

"It's okay," Batgirl assured her. "Really."

Katana stood still, sword in hand as her eyes narrowed.

"Oops," Cyborg said, spilling his chocolate milk shake all over Captain Cold's plate. "My bad!"

He high-fived Katana as Ratcatcher howled with laughter and Captain Cold seethed.

Batgirl smiled, but inside she felt awful. Why did people like Captain Cold have to be jerks? And did her friends really think they had to defend her?

Batgirl found herself on the covers of *Tech* and *Superstar Super Heroes* magazines. Plus, there was a huge feature interview by Lois Lane on the reporter's vlog. Batgirl was the talk of the broadcast media. But it was all talk *about* her. Few in the media bothered to talk *to* her. *Super Hero Hotline,* featuring two former child super heroes as hosts, led with her story.

"It's all about Batgirl," said the woman with the tall orange hair. Her teeth were a blinding white, offset by her bright red lipstick.

"The year of the Bat!" her cohost chimed in. With a few deft moves, he fashioned his impressive mustache to look like a bat.

The weekend rushed toward her. Soon it was time for her to head home. As she hauled her laundry bag through the side door, she wondered if her father would even mention the competition.

"Congratulations!" Commissioner Gordon beamed.

She smiled. So he did know after all! "Thanks, Dad!"

"You know what that means, don't you?" he asked, handing her the detergent.

"What?"

"With the *TechTalkTV* win, everyone knows how great you are. Now you can probably snag any high-tech job you want after college."

Batgirl turned on the washing machine. It made a comforting *chug-chug, chug-chug* sound. "Dad," she said, feeling deflated, "I don't want to work in an office or a lab, I want to be a super hero. Wasn't there something you really wanted when you were a kid?"

He nodded. "Yes. I always wanted to be a police officer."

"Okay, then!" Batgirl said. They were finally getting somewhere. "Your job is dangerous, so I don't see why you don't want me to have one that could be, too."

"This is different," he said. "Barbara, we've talked about this."

Both were silent.

"Barda is doing really well in my class," her father finally said. "Her last paper, 'Crime and Punishment and Perps,' was excellent!"

Finally, Batgirl grumbled, "Great. Applause for Big Barda."

Batgirl didn't want to admit it, but she was happy to be back at school and in the dorms on Monday. Batty seemed more content in the Bat-Bunker, too.

"She's pretty much the best bat in the world," Beast Boy said. Batgirl had to agree. He changed into a bat and started playing tag with Batty.

Batgirl logged on to her computer as the two whooshed above and around her. Some of the girls thought Beast Boy was a total goofball, but Batgirl didn't feel that way. She especially liked that he could keep a secret about Batty. She would eventually get Batty officially sanctioned as a pet, but she was just too busy right now.

What Batgirl didn't like, however, was all the attention that kept coming her way. Nor did Cheetah, Sapphire, Frost, and some of the others. Batgirl was not immune to the rumors that she believed her own press and was starting to get full of herself.

"An amazing feat!" Doc Magnus exclaimed. He had replayed Batgirl's triumphant win for the class. Many yawned. "Truly, incredibly amazing. We could all learn from her."

Batgirl felt her stomach tighten. The subjective votes had put her over the top, not the hard numbers. Had it not been for the audience, Noah Kuttler would have been champ and the spotlight would be on him.

After class, Batgirl retreated to the library. She was supervising the digitization of the cross-reference index, incorporating books and other media. With the help of Supergirl's lightning-fast speed, Batgirl was able to do a clean sweep of duplicate and antiquated books, coming across several written by current teachers, like Dr. Arkham. The school therapist had autographed his books with a large, flashy signature punctuated with a happy face.

Other Supers pitched in to help. Amassing volunteer hours was part of the Super Hero High curriculum, and many preferred working in the library to mowing the hero ball field or relocating old buildings. Several of the binders contained time-sensitive material, so Katana set about slicing and dicing those that had expired by using her sword as a shredder, then handing the piles of paper to Poison Ivy for recycling. Meanwhile, Green Lantern and Supergirl rearranged the bookshelves as Batgirl installed the new media tracking system Star Sapphire's parents had donated.

"Pretty impressive," Harley said as she videoed the library transformation. "Hey, Batgirl, can you help me out with something?"

Batgirl finished installing a new circuit board into one of the older computers. "Sure," she said. "What can I do for you?"

"I want you to help me take Harley's Quinntessentials to the next level," Harley said as she started pressing random buttons on the keyboard. "Beep-beep! Beep-beep!" she said, laughing.

"Please don't do that," Batgirl said, moving the keyboard

away from her. "What do you mean by 'the next level'?"

"Total world media domination," Harley said modestly. "We can work on the rest of the universe after that. Can you help get me there? I thought if I did something high-tech-y, it would give me an edge."

Batgirl thought about it. Total world media domination was a lot to ask. "Maybe," she said, "I can increase your Web channel's popularity threefold."

"That'll do for now," Harley said.

CHAPTER 21

Batgirl was nervous. A boy in a Gotham High jacket at Capes & Cowls kept staring at her.

"Hi, Batgirl!" Steve Trevor called. "Care for a free sample of our new organic carrot cake?"

She took a sample from his tray. It was delish.

"I'll have a slice and a glass of milk," she said.

After Steve brought it over, Batgirl noticed the boy across the room still looking at her. She bent her head when he headed toward her table.

"Don't I know you?" the boy asked.

Batgirl recognized Phil Baker. She had tutored him in math when she went to Gotham High. Despite his fear of complex equations, she helped him bring his grade up from a C- to a B+.

"I don't think so," Batgirl said. She wondered what he wanted.

"It *is* you!" Phil exclaimed. "What are you doing here?"

"Eating?" She hunched over, hoping there weren't any other Gotham High students around.

"Hey, everyone, look who's here!" Phil yelled excitedly. He pointed right at her. "It's Batgirl from that TV show!"

Batgirl tried unsuccessfully not to blush as she waved at the students and even signed a few autographs. She still wasn't used to being in the public eye. Though it was flattering to be recognized, she preferred her Barbara Gordon days, when she could drop by Capes & Cowls and sip a smoothie in peace. Batgirl had to laugh at this memory, though. Because back then, she was probably the only person to never go completely gaga over seeing the super heroes in person, often sitting at the next table.

"Want to join us?" Cyborg asked Batgirl. He was sitting in a booth with Green Lantern and Hawkgirl.

"No thanks," Batgirl said, scanning the room. "I'm meeting someone." She waved at the boy standing in the doorway. "Over here."

"Hey!" he called as he made his way across the café.

"Everyone, this is Noah Kuttler. He was on *TechTalkTV*," Batgirl said, introducing him to some of her fans. "I've never met anyone as tech smart as him. Maybe you'd like his autograph, too!"

Noah lit up, but his smile disappeared as quickly as the fans did. Apparently, they didn't want to meet the guy who'd come in second.

"I'm sure they're busy," Batgirl said quickly.

Both looked at the kids lingering at the doorway. Neither said anything as they took seats.

Noah Kuttler's mass of curly hair was shoved under a dark green baseball cap. Batgirl noticed that his T-shirt was on inside out and backward.

"What can I do for you, Batgirl?" he asked as he sat across from her.

"I'm working on a little project that could use your help," she said.

"If it's electronic equipment you need, you could just spend your prize money," Noah reminded her.

"While I still have it," Batgirl said, laughing. "You know how much computer and tech equipment costs!"

Noah nodded. He did know.

A girl's voice from a nearby table floated over to them. "And so I told my mom, why just get one new car when you can get three, each in a different color to match your outfits?"

Cheetah and Frost, who were sitting with Star Sapphire, nodded.

At another table Big Barda and Lady Shiva rolled their eyes.

"Noah, I'm stuck on some of this code," Batgirl said, opening up her tablet. Numbers marched across the screen. "Can you take a look? I'm jumping off from what we created on *TechTalkTV*."

Noah smiled. "I got you covered!" he assured her.

"HarleyGrams will take me to the next level!" Harley said excitedly.

Katana and Bumblebee had stopped by their table at dinner on their way to the library. Wonder Woman was digging into her third helping of lasagna, and Hawkgirl had just finished her tropical-fruit salad, leaving a pile of kiwi on the edge of her plate.

"The patented HarleyGrams will put Harley Quinn right in the room with you," Harley continued. "A tiny 3-D hologram version of me! What could be better than that?"

"I can think of a dozen—" Beast Boy started to say, before Batgirl shushed him.

"Noah helped with the part of the code I couldn't figure out. Now all I have to do is apply it," Batgirl said. "I may also need some special tech, too. To stay on the cutting edge, you've got to keep up with the latest trends and equipment. Creativity can only take you so far. Then you have to have the hardware."

"Please lower your voices," Star Sapphire said from a nearby table. "No one wants to hear about your hammer and nails."

Back in the Bat-Bunker, Batty was soaring around the room, diving and swooping like Beast Boy had taught her. Batgirl started running the numbers and came to the conclusion she had suspected. There was so much she needed to do, like to finish and upload the HarleyGrams and create all the new B.A.T. gadgets she wanted. But how could she do it all without compromising?

Sure, there was the *TechTalkTV* money, but Batgirl had the good sense not to spend it all; she'd invested some of it for later. Her father would be proud.

"What am I supposed to do, Batty?" she asked. The little bat perched on her shoulder. "To be on the top of the tech world takes funding. There are so many extra things I want to do—not just for me, but for the school, for Harley, for the world!"

The familiar chime of an email landing in her in-box sounded. Batgirl looked. This one had passed the strong spam filter she had created. Ever since she'd won the *TechTalkTV* competition, she'd gotten hundreds of emails a day, most from people wanting something or selling something.

This message was from the Metropolis National Bank and encrypted with a legitimate security code. She clicked Open.

Not believing her eyes, Batgirl pressed the button on her com bracelet. "Supergirl," she whispered. "Can you come to the Bat-Bunker immediately?"

Before she finished her last word, Supergirl was standing next to her saying, "I've never seen so many zeros."

"I know!" Batgirl replied. "And it looks legit."

Supergirl's eyes grew big. "Who do you think sent you the money?"

"I'm trying to figure that out myself," Batgirl said as she input the codes from the bank and ran them through her computer.

"I got it!" Supergirl shouted so loudly that the room reverberated. "I bet you have a tech angel, someone who saw you on the TV show!"

"The note says that the funds are to remain secret or I forfeit them," Batgirl said. She stared at the long list of numbers and letters her computer was coming up with and tried to decipher it. Suddenly, she let out a gasp.

"What is it?" Supergirl asked.

"I know who sent the money," Batgirl said as she double-checked her findings.

"Who?" Supergirl asked. "Is it that producer from the TV show? I bet it's her!"

Batgirl shook her head. "I can't say," she explained. "It's supposed to be an anonymous gift."

"Your secret is safe with me, Batgirl," Supergirl assured her. "Er . . . especially since I don't know who it is!"

"Thank you," Batgirl said. "And now, if you'll excuse me, I have some HarleyGrams to create!"

CHAPTER 22

"**F**ood, food, food!"

Batgirl looked down at her com bracelet. She couldn't believe how much time had passed. "Hello?" Supergirl was saying. "Can you hear me, Batgirl? It's time for dinner. Dinnertime!"

The noise level in the dining hall was almost crushing. Dinner was always more rambunctious than lunch, since classes were over for the day and everyone was eager to decompress. But before the cafeteria ladies could ladle the Super Surprise Stew onto Batgirl's plate, the room began to shake violently.

Everyone went into defense mode. Seconds later, as the alarm sounded, Bumblebee was flying through the dining hall announcing, "Save the Day Alarm! This is not a drill. Repeat, this is NOT a drill. Earthquake in Metropolis. Buildings down! People hurt! All Supers to the city, NOW!"

The Supers scattered, each heading to different quadrants

of Metropolis, as they had been trained to do. Racing to the garage, Batgirl leapt onto one of the motorcycles. She secured her helmet, then sped downtown. She was able to access the police scanner on her B.A.T. computer watch. Morris's Sure-Enuf Shoe Repair was her first stop.

"Mr. Morris, are you okay?" Batgirl called as she ran inside. She didn't let the heavy dust and debris stop her. When she flipped on her Accelerated Amplification Device, she heard a cough and followed it. An elderly man was trapped beneath a mountain of shoes. Instantly, Batgirl began to free him.

"Are you hurt?" she asked.

"No!" Mr. Morris wheezed.

"That's good," she said.

"NO!" he yelled. The sides of his mouth curled downward and there was insult in his eyes. "Not *you!*"

Batgirl stopped.

"In my day, super heroes could fly and move buildings, and were all men. NOT GIRLS!" Mr. Morris grumbled.

Batgirl continued to remove the shoes, then lent a hand to help him up.

"Next time," he grumbled, "I want a real super hero, not a girl."

As Batgirl continued rescuing people, most of whom were far more grateful than Mr. Morris, she tried not to let him get to her. Was she not a "real super hero"? Was she trying to fool everyone, including herself? Batgirl watched as Wonder

Woman and Supergirl teamed up to steady a bridge that threatened to collapse with rush hour traffic still on it. Over at the zoo, Beast Boy was leading the escaped animals back to their habitats. Katana was cutting through the trees that blocked the roads, and Cyborg was hauling them away. It looked like the superpowered heroes had everything under control.

"I am cheating! I am cheating! I AM CHEATING!" All over the school, computers were broadcasting on full volume, "I am cheating!"

"Make it stop!" Cheetah yelled, covering her ears.

"The way to make it stop is not to start," Batgirl tried to tell her and the others. "It's a spam virus!"

Everyone had received the same email. The link promised, "Guaranteed success as a super hero!" Who wouldn't want to click on a link like that, especially since it looked like the emails had come from Vice Principal Grodd's office? But when you clicked on the link, "CHEATER! CHEATER! CHEATER!" bellowed in Grodd's gravelly voice.

And it wasn't just this. Other computer jokes were making the rounds at school. Naturally, suspicion focused on Beast Boy, who was known for his oversized sense of humor, like the time he said he was thirsty, then turned into a camel and drained the punch bowl at Star Sapphire's birthday party extravaganza.

"We'll get to the bottom of this," Hawkgirl said as the rest of the Junior Detective Society nodded.

"Not to worry, Batgirl," Poison Ivy assured her. "We've got it handled."

"Yes, you deal with the computers, we'll find the culprit," The Flash said.

The thing was, Batgirl wanted to help capture the culprit, too. Her father always said that one of the most rewarding parts of being police commissioner was catching the bad guys. Batgirl wished she were a member of the Junior Detective Society. But that was one club you couldn't just sign up for. You had to be invited.

Still, there was plenty to do. With the email spam taking over, it seemed like everyone, students and teachers alike, needed Batgirl's help. She was glad Cyborg's computer skills allowed him to help her prioritize the real emergencies from the false ones.

"Is everything okay?" Principal Waller asked. She had made it a point to check in with Batgirl at least once or twice a week.

"Sure!" Batgirl said brightly. She made a serious effort to look happy and carefree. "Everything is good. No, wait—it's great!"

Waller frowned. "I know everyone is asking for your tech help. I also know the teachers are piling on the assignments right now for midterm grades. And I've heard that you're taking on special projects, like one for a student who happens to have her own video Web channel. That seems like an awful lot to me."

Batgirl was silent for a moment. What could she say? Waller was right.

"Please don't tell my dad," she begged.

Waller arched an eyebrow. "If you can handle it all, I won't. But the minute I think you're overloaded, I will bring this up with your father."

Batgirl nodded. What Waller was saying wasn't a threat, it was a promise.

"Clearly you're stressed," Supergirl said. They were in PE climbing up a fire tower that was, well, on fire.

Luckily, Supergirl had super-hearing and could hear Batgirl from inside the pyroproof face mask and full-body gear protecting her.

"I'm not stressed!" Batgirl said.

From the ground, Catwoman and Barda began throwing stones, logs, and other debris at them, per Wildcat's orders.

"This isn't a dance!" the coach shouted. "This is a test of your climbing skills—under pressure. Faster!"

"Well, I think you're overdoing things," Supergirl said. She caught one of the logs and tossed it back down to Barda, who batted it with her Mega Rod, sending it sailing back as if they were playing volleyball.

The fire was hot, but Batgirl was determined to get to the top of the tower and access the water barrel and douse the flames.

"I hope you don't mind, but I've signed you up for a session with Dr. Arkham," Supergirl said nonchalantly.

"What if I do mind?" Batgirl said, trying to tamp down the heat. Arkham? What did she need a counselor for? She was fine. Maybe a tad stressed, but to be sent to Arkham? Really, now. Was that necessary?

At the top of the tower, Batgirl unleashed the water, letting it gush down, and put out the fire with a steamy hiss.

CHAPTER 23

"**I** see from your charts that you have excelled as a student since our first meeting," Dr. Arkham said as he stroked his impressive beard. "You do know why you're here, correct?"

"Yes." Batgirl hoped this wouldn't take long. She didn't want to miss Liberty Belle's history class. They were having a test, and she could use the relaxation of a test.

"People think I'm stressed," she told him. "But really, I'm not. Okay, okay, maybe a little. Sometimes. But not all the time. Not when I'm asleep!" She let out a too-loud laugh. Batgirl kept dreaming about all the things she was supposed to get done and would wake up exhausted.

"I suppose I should try to slow down, maybe just a bit," she mused aloud. "But perhaps the solution would be to prioritize better. Not to ignore anything, but to categorize into A, B, and C sections, A being 'Get it done now,' B being 'Important, but it won't kill you to wait a bit,' and C being, 'Get to it when you can.'"

Dr. Arkham kept nodding, sometimes with his eyes closed. Batgirl continued. "Everyone thinks they're the only ones having a tech crisis. Maybe if I had them fill out a form, they'd have to slow down and think instead of running to me at the first sign of trouble."

Batgirl spoke faster and faster as new plans started to form. By the end of the session, she felt much better. "Thank you, Dr. Arkham. You're amazing!" she said.

He started to speak but stopped himself. After all, Batgirl had done all the talking, and this had been one of his most productive counseling sessions of the week!

"Oh," Batgirl added as she was leaving his office. "My HarleyGrams are set to debut soon. They've been taking up a ton of my life. But once they're up and running, I'll have a lot of free time."

"WOWZA! BAM! BOOM! I'm LOVING it!"

Batgirl couldn't help being thrilled by Harley's enthusiasm. She had worked so hard on the HarleyGrams, and now, at last, they weren't just computer codes, they were real!

"Here's what you do," a video of Harley was saying on the screen. They had logged on to the Harley's Quinntessentials home page. "Just click on my face and instantly a HarleyGram will pop up on your computer keyboard. Then wait for the fun to begin!"

"Shall we try it?" Harley asked. Her eyes were shining.

"You do the honors," Batgirl said generously.

"Here we go!" Harley cried as she dramatically clicked the mouse.

Almost instantly, a little hologram of Harley Quinn appeared on the keyboard. It did flips and jumps as it ran back and forth across the keys, waving a mallet, and yelling, "Harley's Quinntessentials!"

"This is amazing," Harley said. Lois Lane was doing a feature on the latest craze to sweep the country. "My HarleyGrams have been available for less than a week and nearly half a million people have downloaded them!"

"Did you create this yourself?" Lois Lane asked.

"Well, it was pretty much all my idea," Harley bragged as she leapt up and did a flip. "That's right! Who's right? Harley! WOWZA!"

Batgirl didn't say anything when she saw the interview.

"It was you," Katana pointed out. "Not her."

"It's okay," Batgirl said. "Seriously, I've had enough of the spotlight to last me a couple of decades. I'm more than happy to sit this one out."

The anonymity didn't last long. Lois Lane was too excellent a reporter to take anything at face value. She had done a follow-up story about the HarleyGrams, revealing that Batgirl was the brains behind the Internet phenomenon.

Soon *Super Hero Hotline* had devoted a full segment to HarleyGrams with its kooky hosts demonstrating how a HarleyGram works, using a giant keyboard and then running across it yelling and hitting each other with mallets.

Of course, the most press came from Harley herself. She interviewed Wonder Woman, Supergirl, Katana, Poison Ivy, and other students, asking for their "true and real candid opinions about these amazing HarleyGrams!"

"I think they're fun!" Wonder Woman said.

"I've never seen anything like them before—at least, not on Earth," admitted Supergirl.

"A CheetahGram would be better," Cheetah pointed out.

"Is it good for the environment?" Poison Ivy asked. Her interview got cut.

The person Harley forgot to interview was Batgirl. But that didn't detract from the attention she was getting. Soon major tech companies wanted to hire her immediately. HarleyGrams were the must-have toy, and Batgirl was lauded for her high-tech skills. When she refused all interviews, it only made her more mysterious and thus more sought after.

Despite her protests, Batgirl was now a full-blown media star, and with the spotlight shining brightly on her, she could barely see past it.

CHAPTER 24

The next week swept past in a blur. Batgirl was busy with her schoolwork and troubleshooting assorted tech problems. The library installation had gone well. Now students were able to access books and resource material from their dorm rooms, space vehicles, anywhere—though many still congregated at the heavy wooden tables in the library that were lit with old-fashioned green banker's lamps.

"It feels so awesomely retro and academic to study in here," Hawkgirl whispered.

"I know!" Batgirl agreed. "I know . . . but this is where all the knowledge is. I love the smell of information in this room." Just as she was about to sniff an old leather-bound copy of Ra's al Ghul's *The Decline of the Ancient World,* someone cried, "THERE YOU ARE!"

Everyone looked up to see Harley holding her mallet in the air as if ready to strike.

"Batgirl," she yelled. "I need to talk to you, NOW!"

Instinctively, Batgirl shushed her. Everyone knew to keep their voice down in the library. "What is it?" she asked as she rushed Harley into the hallway.

"The HarleyGrams have gone *bonkers*!" Harley blurted out. She could not stop jumping up and down.

"Explain," Batgirl said evenly. She was an expert at calming people down. When it came to computer issues, people often lost control. A recalcitrant computer could bring even the toughest heroes close to tears.

"I'm getting complaints that some of the HarleyGrams are running back and forth on the keyboards, changing what people are typing," Harley said. "Then the HarleyGram takes out her mallet and WHAM! She uses it to hit random computer keys! *Random keys!* WHAM!"

Batgirl shook her head. This couldn't be happening! "Wait. Slow down, Harley," she said. "Are you telling me that the HarleyGrams are physically hitting the keyboards?"

Harley nodded. Batgirl felt weak. It wasn't possible. How could a hologram do that? They were just computer-generated light projections.

"How many computers have been affected?" she asked. "Is it a confined area or widespread?"

"So far the complaints are just at school. Can you fix it? Batgirl, you have to fix it. People are getting mad at me!"

The two hurried over to the Bat-Bunker. Luckily, Batty was a heavy sleeper; otherwise Harley's yelling would have startled her awake. Batgirl sneakily moved her to the closet so Harley wouldn't see her.

"Please," Batgirl said as Harley bounced off the walls. Literally. "If you want me to fix this, you're going to have to stay still and be quiet."

Batgirl fired up her computers. The screens bathed the room in blue light. Harley's face turned red while she held her breath in an effort to remain silent. Batgirl logged on, then checked the HarleyGram Comments/Praise/Complaints email account. Sure enough, there were dozens of complaints. Cheetah and Star Sapphire had taken videos of their HarleyGrams running amok. Star Sapphire had sent a scathing letter threatening to sue. Miss Martian apologized and then asked how to fix it.

"I'm going to disable the HarleyGrams," Batgirl said. "That means no one else can download one until I figure out what's gone wrong. It could just be a minor programming error. Luckily, it seems confined to Super Hero High."

Harley exhaled. "So you're gonna fix it, right?"

"I'm going to try," Batgirl assured her. "Um, if you don't mind, I can get more done when I'm alone."

"Got it!" Harley said, nodding sagely.

Batgirl looked at her. "Harley, that means leave."

"Oooooh," Harley said. "Call me when it's fixed!"

"Hey, do me a favor," Batgirl said when Harley was almost

out the door. "Can you ask Cyborg to come to the Bat-Bunker? Tell him I need tech assistance ASAP!"

Batgirl stayed up deep into the night. She looked up every Super Hero High student who had downloaded a HarleyGram—and that was almost everyone. Then, one by one, she examined the accessed files. She had noticed that on those computers with a rogue HarleyGram, the codes had a tiny variation from the others. But how did it get there? And how did a hologram turn into solid matter?

Cyborg paced the room while tapping on his forehead. It made a light metal-on-metal sound. Just as Batgirl was going to ask him to stop, he faced her and said, "I've got it! The HarleyGrams are going through some sort of high-tech evolution . . . ," he began.

"Of course!" Batgirl added. "Like what we learned in Doc Magnus's class about computer-generated artificial intelligence. They started as holograms but are embedded with an encrypted virus capable of learning on its own. Now they're able to morph into something more substantial, transitioning from a photographic light field into an energy matrix approximating solid matter."

"We're thinking the same thing," Cyborg chimed in. "But how is this happening?"

Batgirl took a deep breath, then said, "That, I don't know."

"Did you fix it? Did you fix it?" Harley asked at breakfast. She was so excited she couldn't sit. Instead, she kept circling the table with her video camera on.

Batgirl was getting dizzy. And she was exhausted. Luckily, there were no big assignments due that day.

"It was really weird," Cyborg said. He set his tray down at Batgirl's table. "I mean, one minute the HarleyGram was just standing on the keyboard waving, and the next it was as if you—I mean, *it* had gone crazy!"

Harley scowled. "Hopefully, the press hasn't picked up on this," she said. "It would be really bad for business."

Batgirl nodded and bit into a piece of dry toast. She was too tired to spread her favorite blueberry jam, made from Poison Ivy's garden. Batgirl wondered what Lois Lane and everyone who had interviewed her would think if they ever found out that the HarleyGrams weren't perfect.

"Batgirl," Bumblebee said, interrupting Liberty Belle's class. "Principal Waller would like to see you in her office."

When Batgirl reached the office, The Wall was waiting for her. There wasn't much that could scare Batgirl, but when she saw the serious look on Amanda Waller's face, her mouth went dry.

"We're getting reports about the HarleyGrams," the

principal began, not even bothering to say hello.

Batgirl let out a sigh of relief and sank into the chair across from Waller's desk. It was piled high with files and confiscated weapons. "Oh, those!" she exclaimed. "I know all about that, and they're fixed now."

The principal turned her computer so that it faced Batgirl. "This is what you already know about? I don't see how you could have fixed it, because it's happening right now."

Batgirl stared at the screen, transfixed. What she was seeing was impossible!

The video showed a little HarleyGram—once a hologram, but now an autonomous electromagnetic figure running across the keyboard, then raising its mallet high in the air. In one swift motion, it brought the mallet down and—WHAM!— hit a random computer key, messing up the computer. But it got worse. Other videos revealed that when a Bad HarleyWham hit the shift key, it unlocked a computer virus. Soon HarleyWhams were shutting down websites, locking keyboards, wiping out emails, and more. And it wasn't just at Super Hero High. Slowly, reports began filtering in that the virus was spreading outside the school.

"What do you think is the cause of this?" Doc Magnus asked as he entered the room, already aware of the situation. As the Robotics and Computer Science teacher, he was the most skilled faculty member when it came to complex technical issues.

"I have no clue," Batgirl admitted. Her stomach clenched, and she felt like doubling over. She was used to fixing things, not destroying them.

"It's not your fault," Cyborg said as Batgirl sat in her room going over and over the computer code. He had brought her some sandwiches since she had skipped lunch. Supergirl had brought sandwiches, too, and Bumblebee, Wonder Woman, and Hawkgirl had all dropped off lunch, as well.

"This is horrible!" Harley hollered as she ran up and down the walls in the Bat-Bunker. "People are making fun of me! They're saying it's all my fault, when really, it's all *your* fault. It can't get any worse than this. OH NO!" Harley looked at Batgirl. "It just did get worse!"

Batgirl froze.

"Apparently, when a HarleyWham, the corrupted version of the HarleyGram, hits a certain sequence of keys, it creates a duplicate HarleyGram," Lois Lane was reporting live on her vlog. "The once-harmless HarleyGrams are now duplicating, and it seems they are intent on taking down the Internet. Can they be stopped?" she asked, looking straight into the camera.

Batgirl knew she was talking to her.

"It's okay," Supergirl said, putting an arm around her.

Batgirl walked away from her. "It's not okay," she said. "This *is* somehow my fault!"

"It's not your fault," Cyborg repeated.

"Something has gone wrong," Supergirl said, trying to console her. "You didn't do this on purpose."

"Listen," Batgirl told her. "I am responsible for this. I got us into this. I have to get us out of this."

"That's true," Harley jumped in. "It's all her fault."

"Well, you wanted the HarleyGrams," Supergirl reminded Harley.

"Stop it!" Batgirl heard herself saying. "Supergirl, please let me take responsibility for my mistakes. All of you, please— let me handle this."

Supergirl nodded and quietly exited the room.

Batgirl was too busy scouring the Internet to notice that her best friend wasn't in the Bat-Bunker anymore, and Harley and Cyborg were gone, too. Suddenly, something caught her attention.

Batgirl gasped. It felt like someone had punched her in the stomach. Blogs, vlogs, and news reports were starting to appear, questioning the HarleyGrams/HarleyWhams. There were several unsubstantiated theories. The most prevalent one was there was a new criminal in town, a mastermind who had created the virus.

That person's name was Batgirl.

PART
THREE

CHAPTER 25

"Barbara?"

Her father seemed surprised to see her on a school night.

"I was in a hurry and forgot my key." Batgirl stood on the front porch with her suitcases by her side. "May I come in?"

"Yes, of course. Of course," Commissioner Gordon said, stepping aside.

"I suppose you know why I'm here," she said. The house smelled faintly like onions and garlic.

"I have my suspicions," her father said. "I was just making myself dinner. Why don't you join me and tell me what's going on."

"Dad," she began, starting to choke up, "I—I—I don't know . . ."

He reached out and gave her a hug. "It's okay, Babs," he said. "You're home now."

Oh, how she had missed her dad's hugs. It felt great.

Batgirl was mostly silent during dinner as she poked at

her meat loaf. She wasn't very hungry.

"I thought I was doing something good—or at least fun—by creating the HarleyGrams," she confessed. "But everything has gone so wrong. It's not just the school. The virus has spread to Metropolis and beyond. Everyone is blaming me, and the horrible thing is that it's my fault the Internet is being corrupted."

"Barbara," her father began. She braced herself, waiting for a lecture. If there was ever a time she deserved one, it was now. She knew he would tell her that she should have never enrolled in Super Hero High.

"Yes?" she said meekly.

"What do you say I make some of my famous peanut butter pecan popcorn? I know it's your favorite."

Batgirl allowed a smile to alight on her face—the first time she'd smiled in days.

"That would be great, Dad," Batgirl said, adding, "Would you mind if I move back home?"

It was weird but comforting not going to school. Batgirl knew that eventually she would have to return to either Super Hero High or Gotham High, but for now, she was content to stay in her pajamas all day and watch television—and let her subconscious do the work. She'd had no idea that there was an entire channel devoted to baby animals (that was

Batty's favorite) and another one that showed nothing but reruns of a series about a wacky stay-at-home dad and his even wackier triplets, Larry, Mary, and Perry. Plus, there was a music channel that played endless videos by her favorite band, Birds of Prey.

Batgirl found herself with a lot of free time. In the beginning it made her anxious, but she could tell the freedom was allowing her mind to process her situation. The answer was deep in her noggin—somewhere. She just needed to let that answer find its way to the surface.

And in the meantime, she appreciated that her father didn't lecture her or say I told you so. In fact, he acted like nothing had happened.

The two talked over dinner, but not about school or work. Instead, Batgirl filled him in on Mary, Larry, and Perry's latest hijinks and what Birds of Prey videos she'd seen. And he told her about the weather. Still, it was nice to be talking to her dad again. He was the only person she spoke to. Well, him and Batty.

Batgirl had made a conscious effort to avoid all media, including computers, phones, and even her com bracelet, the one she had made and shared with Supergirl so they would never have to be apart.

"Barbara," her father said one morning. She had been at home for three days. "I'll probably have to work late tonight, so you'll be on your own for dinner. There's a cyber-crime crisis that seems to be getting big— Never mind."

Batgirl looked up from the television. She had watched all the shows she could find—documentaries, talk-show interviews, bits of gossip about the Birds of Prey and was now rewatching them.

"Cyber crime?" Batgirl asked.

"Forget I even said anything," he told her, waving his hand in the air as if it would erase his words. "There are leftover meatballs in the fridge, and there's peppermint cookie crunch ice cream in the freezer. And, Barbara," he added, "if you need anything, anything at all, just call me."

She nodded and then turned her attention back to the television.

A few moments later, she heard a knock and was surprised to see Supergirl floating at the window. There was a second knock, this one coming from the front door.

"Katana?" Batgirl asked when she opened the door.

Katana didn't look happy. Supergirl appeared behind her.

"You're not answering my phone calls," Katana said, stepping into the house.

"You're not even answering our com bracelets," Supergirl said. "Hey, is that pecan popcorn?"

"Yeah, we've been making it a lot the last few days. What

are you doing here?" Batgirl asked. She was secretly glad to see her friends.

"What aren't YOU doing here?" Katana asked. "There's a world to save!"

"Have you been keeping up with what's going on?" Supergirl said.

"Well, noooo," Batgirl admitted.

Katana picked up the TV remote and changed the channel. Batgirl could not believe what she saw unfolding before her.

"International businesses, governments, the national economy, the space program, vending machines, automated parking meters, even animatronic mice at kids' party restaurants have all been affected," the serious-looking newscaster was saying. He lowered his glasses. "All this because of the viruses caused by the HarleyWhams. We now have this exclusive interview with Harley Quinn. Harley, what do you have to say for yourself?"

Batgirl sat down, disbelieving, as Harley's familiar face showed up on-screen.

"I am innocent!" Harley proclaimed. "The HarleyGrams weren't my idea."

"Then whose idea were they?" the newscaster asked, looking into the camera and frowning.

"They were Batgirl's idea. All her idea," Harley said. "She created them, and now that they're HarleyWhams, well, I had nothing to do with that, either!"

"Do you know where Batgirl is and if she's addressing this situation?" the newscaster asked. On the screen behind him, a photo of Batgirl and Noah Kuttler at the *TechTalkTV* show appeared. The camera slowly zoomed in on Batgirl's face so that it filled the screen.

"I have no idea where she is," Harley said. She looked directly into the camera. "Where are you, Batgirl?" Harley held up her own camera and pushed it right into the screen.

CHAPTER 26

Batgirl couldn't ignore Katana's and Supergirl's stares any longer.

"Well?" Katana asked as Batgirl took note of her samurai warrior costume. She always looked sleek and put-together. "Are you going to just let this happen?"

"Batgirl, the world is becoming a jumble," Supergirl said. "Lives are in danger! We're doing all we can to help, but it keeps getting worse."

Batgirl changed the channel back to the Birds of Prey concert she'd been watching.

"Batgirl!" Supergirl shouted. "Only you can stop this virus!"

"All the Supers have fanned out and are directing traffic, rescuing people and thwarting crime caused by the computer malfunctions," Katana said above the Birds of Prey, who were now singing their hit "Frequent Flyers." She took the remote from Batgirl and turned to another channel. "Look!"

Batgirl watched, expressionless. The Flash was running around a broken dam, fixing several leaks in the process. Wonder Woman put a rocket back on course. Hawkgirl was calming a mob of unruly senior citizens, who were complaining that their computers had frozen and they couldn't play video bingo.

"Batgirl," Supergirl implored. "You're the only one who can reverse the HarleyWhams!"

Batgirl's lips pursed. She wished Katana and Supergirl would leave her alone—just for a little while. That thing that was stirring in her subconscious was getting close to the surface now.

Batgirl turned the television to mute. Silence filled the room.

"Please go away," she said. Her voice was flat.

"Batgirl," Supergirl implored. "We need you. The world needs you!"

"Come on, Supergirl," Katana said, heading to the door. "I thought she was one of us, but apparently I was wrong."

Batgirl stood alone in the living room. The television was still on mute, but she could see the scenes of carnage unfolding. Suddenly, the itch in the back of her brain got a lot stronger, and now she was going to scratch it.

"This is all my fault," Batgirl told Batty later. "But what am I supposed to do? How can I fix what I don't know how to fix?"

The little bat flew around the bedroom before hiding under a blanket.

"I wish my life were as simple as yours," Batgirl said, her thoughts actually starting to move faster. "You're never in a hurry. But I went too fast. I was in such a rush to deliver something spectacular, something the world had never seen before. Instead of trusting myself and my testing methods, I reached out to Noah to help me create the code. I should have slowed down. Beta-tested, double-tested, triple-, quadruple-tested, but instead . . ."

Batgirl stopped. "I reached out to Noah Kuttler," she repeated softly. "Noah. Of course! He helped me with the code. The code we started creating when we were the tech teens on *TechTalkTV.* That code is the key to all this!"

Batgirl rooted around in her desk drawer, finally finding what she was looking for. "Supergirl," she called into her com bracelet. "Come back!"

Before she could repeat herself, Supergirl was standing in her room. Katana came running in a few moments later.

"I know what happened," she said in a rush. "It's Noah Kuttler!"

"That nerdy kid?" Katana asked.

"That tech genius," Batgirl told her. "My partner from the TV show. The destructive code from the HarleyWhams must have been programmed and embedded in the HarleyGrams from the outset. I didn't have the full code created, so I met with Noah at Capes and Cowls Café and he helped me with it! When I asked if we should test it, he assured me it would work. 'Why wait?' he said."

Katana was already heading toward the door. "Come on, Supergirl," she called. "Let's alert the others and take this criminal down!"

"No!" Batgirl said. "Don't tell anyone just yet. Let me handle this!"

"Are you sure?" Supergirl asked.

"I'm sure," Batgirl said. "You two help the other Supers keep the damage to a minimum while I figure out how to handle Noah. I don't want him to know we're on to him."

Katana shook her head. "I don't agree with you, Batgirl," she said. "But I trust that you know what you're doing."

For the first time in days, Batgirl turned on her computer. It didn't take her long to find Noah. His name and address were in the AboutFace database. With Batty watching, she contacted him, and was shocked by what she saw.

"Well, hello, Batgirl," Noah said. "What took you so long?"

Batgirl did a double-take. Gone was the nerdy kid she had known. In his place was a confident teenage boy wearing a deep purple turtleneck with even purpler jeans and a black jacket that had computer circuitry woven into it. Computer keys and sophisticated inputs of various kinds ran up and down each sleeve. And to top off his sinister look, he had tamed his unruly hair into an elegant coiffure. He wore an evil sneer and wire-rim tech glasses on his face. It was a makeover to best all makeovers.

"Hello, Noah," Batgirl said evenly. Staying calm is your best weapon, her father always said.

His jaw tightened as he turned up the collar of his jacket so that it framed his head. "I'm not Noah. Noah doesn't live here anymore. I'm the Calculator!"

He let out a long, evil laugh. It sounded practiced.

"No, you're Noah Kuttler," Batgirl corrected him.

"Right," he spit back. "And you're Barbara Gordon."

Batgirl winced.

"How do you know who I am?" she asked.

"There's not much about you that I don't know," he said mysteriously.

The two tech teens stared at each other from their respective computer screens. This would be a test, Batgirl knew. Of a potential super hero and a potential super-villain.

"What do you want . . . Calculator?" Batgirl asked.

He smiled as the circuitry in his jacket pulsed and blinked. "Hmmmm . . . what do I want? Maybe I want to take down the Internet and accelerate the virus and BRING THE EARTH TO A SCREECHING HALT!"

Batgirl wondered why he felt the need to scream.

"Why would you want to do that?" she asked.

"Why would you want to hog all the glory from the *TechTalkTV* show? If you hadn't insisted on bringing your entire Super Hero High school to the show and throwing the votes, I would be champion, not you!"

Batgirl sat in stunned silence. Was that what this was all about? A vendetta? The Calculator didn't want to just destroy the world. He wanted to hurt her. Batgirl reached for her com bracelet.

"Oops, bad Internet connection," Batgirl told him, shutting off AboutFace. She spoke into her bracelet. "Supergirl, can you come back?"

Supergirl tapped Batgirl on the shoulder.

"Could you at least knock when you do that?" Batgirl asked, startled.

"What's going on?" Supergirl said.

"It's worse than I thought," Batgirl told her. "Noah—he's calling himself the Calculator—is the smartest tech person in the world."

"Correction," Supergirl said. "You are. You beat him on the TV show."

"No . . . ," Batgirl said slowly. "He won two out of the three competitions. I only won because all of you and the studio audience and judges voted for me after he did that ridiculous dance. If we went strictly by the numbers, he would be champion."

"Not really . . . You won two contests and came in second

on one. Kuttler only won two contests. This wasn't just a popularity contest! You deserved your win! What does this have to do with the virus, anyway?" asked Supergirl.

"It has everything to do with it," Batgirl explained. "He wants to prove that he's better than me and that I can't stop him."

Batty flew around the room and snuggled into Batgirl's hand.

"But you can stop him, right?" Supergirl asked.

"I'm not so sure," Batgirl said, stroking Batty's tummy. "He's brilliant."

"So are *you*," her best friend said. "What true super heroes have in common is their ability to *try*, even in the face of overwhelming odds."

Batgirl didn't know what to say. Supergirl went on, "How do you think I felt when my planet was destroyed and I lost my parents? I wanted to quit. I really, really did, because I felt so alone. But the Kents and Wonder Woman and everyone else—especially *you*, Batgirl—told me that I needed to go on. That I was to be defined not by what I lost, but by what I had to offer. Now I'm telling you the same thing.

"Batgirl, you have so much potential and power. You owe it to yourself, you owe it to me, you owe it to the people you swore to protect when you came to Super Hero High, to help when you can, where you can."

The two best friends stared at each other. Supergirl looked more serious than Batgirl had ever seen her. Batgirl nodded and asked, "How do you feel about crunching numbers?"

"Huh? Crunching numbers? Like doing math?" Supergirl asked.

Batgirl allowed a smile to slowly appear on her face. "I was thinking more like crunching the Calculator?" she said, raising an eyebrow. "POW!"

Supergirl laughed, then held up her hand and said, "I'm right there with you."

And with that, the two best friends high-fived, happy to be back on the world's finest team once more.

CHAPTER 27

"Let's meet back at Super Hero High," Batgirl told Supergirl. "Tell Principal Waller I'm returning. Ask the other Supers to keep doing exactly what they're doing—saving lives and preventing chaos. Except have the Junior Detective Society make a world map isolating where the main damage is being done. And have Cyborg on standby in case I need more computer help."

"Anything else?" Supergirl asked.

"Yeah," said Batgirl sheepishly. "Please accept my apology. I'm sorry I ran and hid, but Batgirl is back now."

Batgirl knew that returning to Super Hero High would cause problems. Not with Principal Waller, who needed her to clean up the mess she had made, but with her father. After all, as part of their agreement, she was to stay away from danger. But she had no choice. There was only one way to stop the potential meltdown of the Internet, and that was to go to the source. Confront the enemy. Get face to face with the Calculator.

Batgirl turned to Batty. "We need to get to the Bat-Bunker. All my equipment is there. I'll fight Calculator tech with Batgirl tech." She looked at the photo of her and her father when she was little. "Sorry, Dad, but there's something I have to do."

With mixed emotions, Batgirl sat down at her desk and pulled out the stationery her father had given her for her birthday. Across the top, in fancy print, was *From the Desk of Barbara Gordon.*

Dear Dad,

I am not asking your permission to fight crime but telling you that it's in my blood—just like it's in yours. Because of something I did, the world is being threatened. It's up to me to fix this. Yes, it may be dangerous. And yes, I am aware of the consequences.

Dad, I love you. You are my role model. You've always told me about the risks of fighting crime, and of the battle of good vs.

evil. You've told me of the dangers ... and the rewards. But most of all, you've taught me that to ignore injustice is a crime itself.

And so, I must do this.

Your loving daughter

She crossed out *Barbara Gordon* at the top of the stationery and wrote *Batgirl,* then placed the letter on her nightstand.

Before she left, there was one more thing to do. Batgirl walked over to her closet and pulled out her Batsuit. As she put it on, she felt an energy surge that she hadn't felt in days.

She looked into the mirror. "Believe in your super self. Believe in your super self," Batgirl repeated over and over, slowly and softly at first, her voice getting stronger and more urgent as she went on.

Finally, she broke into a bold smile. "Watch out, Calculator," she said confidently. "Batgirl is back!"

CHAPTER 28

"**B**atgirl," a loud voice called. "A minute of your time?"

Batgirl froze.

"While I am thrilled to have you back, the circumstances are less than ideal," Waller said sternly. "What do you have to say for yourself?"

"That this is my fault, and that I aim to fix it," Batgirl said. She told Principal Waller all about the Calculator and his evil plan.

Waller held up her hand to stop her. "Batgirl, are you aware of the risks and dangers involved?"

Batgirl nodded. She was. Her teachers had been telling the students about this from day one. Going to Super Hero High was not all flying and fun. Everyone knew the risks. When it came time to rescue, thwart evil, and help the world, everyone had to be focused. They weren't ordinary teens, they were super hero teens who took their roles very seriously.

"I am well aware that danger is involved," Batgirl assured

Waller. "I know how the Calculator thinks, because we're alike in so many ways. There is no one better suited to take him on than I am. I made the mess; let me clean it up."

Waller stood stone-faced. Her eyes narrowed as if she were looking into Batgirl's soul. "I know you, Batgirl," she began. "Maybe even better than you know yourself. You are brave, and bold, and smart. Go get the Calculator. Stop the chaos. Afterward, we'll talk about your future here."

Beast Boy joined Batgirl as she rushed to the Bat-Bunker. She handed him Batty's carrier. Normally, Beast Boy was all jokes and laughs. But not now. Not today.

With each button she pressed, with each toggle she turned on, with each computer that emitted a familiar blue glow, Batgirl felt a new strength running through her body.

"Here," Beast Boy said, handing her a map. "It's from the Junior Detective Society. The Flash and the others are at the Gotham City airport control tower redirecting the planes. The computer system is down, but Cyborg's working on getting it back up and running."

Batgirl unfolded the map. She recognized Poison Ivy's flowery handwriting. The numbers in the legend were clearly Hawkgirl's doing. And the precise coordinates were all The Flash.

"According to this," she told Beast Boy, "the Web meltdowns are all starting somewhere around here."

"How can we stop it?" he asked.

Batty landed on his shoulder as he and Batgirl watched

scenes of confusion on the screens. Big Barda was using her Mega Rod to stop criminals at the Metropolis Bank. "Just because the security system is disabled doesn't mean that gives you freedom to clean out the bank!" she roared, leaping into action.

On another screen, they saw Lady Shiva delivering power generators to the hospital, while on a third screen Cheetah was comforting a group of kindergarteners trapped in the dinosaur room in a museum while on their field trip.

"I'm not sure how to stop it yet," Batgirl said, bringing up a world map on her computer and inputting the information from the Junior Detective Society. With a few keystrokes, points on the map began to glow, showing where the HarleyWhams were causing the most damage.

"By scrambling the computer viruses, we can slow the current chaos," she said, inputting more information. "That'll buy us time. What I have to figure out is how to stop more HarleyWhams from happening."

"It's you!" someone yelled accusingly, pounding on her door.

"Hi, Harley," Batgirl said, her eyes still on the computer. Using a simple reverse AboutFace program, she was locking in on the location the Calculator had broadcast from.

"This is all your fault!" Harley yelled from the other side of the door. She wouldn't go away.

"Yes, I think we've established that," Batgirl said calmly.

"Well, you've got to stop it NOW!" Harley ordered.

"Focus," Beast Boy said. "You can't afford any distractions right now."

Batgirl nodded. "Please secure the Bat-Bunker from the inside," she directed him.

For once, Beast Boy didn't protest and did what he was told. Soon they could hear Harley pounding on the door with her mallet. "Hey!" she cried. "I can't get this door open! Is it broken? Hey! Wha . . . *Oomph!!!*"

Batgirl and Beast Boy looked at each other, then at the broadcast from the security camera outside the Bat-Bunker. Harley was caught in one of the traps that Batgirl had set for intruders and was flailing around in a net suspended in the air.

"Okay," Batgirl said. "Time to get down to business."

CHAPTER 29

It was worse than she had originally thought. Batgirl had managed to slow the damage by isolating the areas where the HarleyWhams had infected computers. As a precaution, she also blasted antivirus software through a series of geosynchronous satellites. Still, she couldn't figure out why the virus was getting worse, not better.

"I don't believe this!" she said, shaking her head. The HarleyWhams were jumping off their keyboards and seeking out new computers.

Beast Boy looked over her shoulder. "Seriously?" he croaked. He had turned himself into a frog and had been leaping up and down to release excess energy as Batty flew around the room. "That's the last thing the world needs right now."

"This is no ordinary virus," Lois Lane was reporting from one of the many computer windows feeding Batgirl information. "This is a full-blown epidemic. The

HarleyWhams must be contained! We caught up with Harley earlier today! A word for my Web viewers?"

On the screen, Harley opened her mouth and nothing came out. She flapped her jaw and tried to speak, but it was as if her volume had been turned to mute. In a panic, she somersaulted away from the camera.

Lois looked into the lens and reported, "Harley's Quinntessentials, at one time the most-subscribed-to video channel, has virtually no viewers left. That's right, Harley Quinn has lost all her viewers. The channel has gone dark."

"Well," Beast Boy kept asking. "Well? Well? Anything? Well?"

There wasn't much to see other than Batgirl sitting in various poses, thinking.

"Are you still . . . ," he began.

"Yes, still thinking," she said, now sitting cross-legged, eyes closed, trying to focus as she had seen Katana do.

There was a loud THUMP outside the door. Batgirl and Beast Boy looked at the security camera feed. Harley was back. She had gotten herself out of the net.

"Hey, Batgirl, let me in! I want to HELP!" she cried.

"Harley helping with computers is like Granny Goodness's Parademons helping in the kitchen," Beast Boy said, referring to the mischievous little scamps that had recently run amok at the school.

"Will you explain to Harley that though I appreciate her offer, she might be a distraction?" Batgirl said.

"A distraction?" Beast Boy snorted. "More like a destruction."

With Beast Boy out of the Bat-Bunker soothing Harley, Batgirl allowed herself to slump in her chair. She had to stop the HarleyWhams, but what she really needed to do was to stop the source of the destruction. And the computer software to do that from a remote location would cost money. Something she was quickly running out of.

Batgirl's stomach began to cramp. It was only then that she realized she had been so busy that she had skipped several meals. She made sure Batty was content and then snuck past Beast Boy and Harley.

As soon as she got to the dining hall, Batgirl scarfed down a couple of ham sandwiches.

Just then, Supergirl flew up. "How's it going, Batgirl?" she asked as Star Sapphire and Cheetah strolled past.

"It's going to take longer than I thought," Batgirl admitted. "I don't have the extra funds to supercharge my Internet defenses. What's happening is big-time. I can still think of a workaround, though."

Batgirl loaded up some more sandwiches and an armful of fruit and headed back to the Bat-Bunker. It was going to be a long night.

As Batgirl sat at the controls, she noticed that the destruction was starting to slow down.

A chime from her private email startled her.

There was a message from the Metropolis National Bank. It was from the anonymous benefactor. Another substantial deposit had been made. Batgirl was ecstatic. This was exactly what she needed. Immediately, she purchased and began to download the programs she could cobble together to create a customized B.A.T. super program to thwart the HarleyWhams.

Another alert from her private email sounded. Happily, she opened the message, thinking it was from the bank again.

Wrong.

> To: Batgirl
>
> From: The Calculator
>
> Subject: You Lose
>
> Message: You think money can get you out of the mess you've created? Well, you're wrong, Batgirl. Have fun watching the Internet self-destruct!

Batgirl was shocked. How did he know about the money? It was as if the Calculator was privy to her private information. Did he have access to bank accounts, too?

Batty flew around the room and then snuggled into Batgirl's lap. "You sweet little thing," she told the baby bat. "I'm glad you aren't aware of what's going on out there."

There was a knock on the door.

"I'm working!" Batgirl yelled, not even bothering to look at the security camera video.

"It's me!" a familiar voice called.

Cyborg was waving to the camera. He was carrying a paper bag. Batgirl pressed a button and buzzed him in.

The door to the Bat-Bunker slid open and then closed, apparently in Harley's face. "Hey!" she yelled as a blinding light flashed.

"I brought you some food," Cyborg said, holding up a bag.

"Thanks," Batgirl said, motioning to her pile of sandwiches. "But I have those."

"But do you have these?" he asked, taking out a smoothie and sweet potato fries from Capes & Cowls Café.

Batgirl couldn't help but smile. "Thanks, Cyborg," she said. Never had a strawberry smoothie tasted so good.

"Anytime," he said. "Okay, gotta get back to my computer. NASA is reporting a satellite shutdown."

Batgirl gave him a weary smile. "I'm glad you're on this with me."

Cyborg smiled back. "And I'm glad you're at Super Hero High. It's nice having a high-tech friend."

Batty was flying around the room again.

"Your bat is cute," Cyborg said. "I think she likes me."

"I think you're right," Batgirl said as Batty slammed into his head.

"Um," Cyborg said awkwardly, "I think your bat is stuck on my face."

Sure enough, she was.

"It's as if she's magnetically drawn to you," Batgirl noted. "Literally."

As she gently pulled, she noticed a teeny tiny lump in Batty's wing. Putting her under a magnifying glass and shining an X-ray light on it, Batgirl saw something startling.

"What's the matter?" Cyborg asked. "Are you okay?"

"I'm fine," Batgirl said loudly. "I just have a splinter. Hey, would you mind asking Beast Boy to come to the Bat-Bunker? Or—wait, never mind. I'll go find him. You stay with Batty."

"Where are you going?" Harley cried, when Batgirl rushed past her.

"To save the world," Batgirl answered. She ran up to Beast Boy and pulled him aside for a private talk.

"You're seriously kidding me!" Beast Boy exclaimed. "Where is she now?"

"Still in the Bat-Bunker with Cyborg," Batgirl told him. "Batty has been microchipped! That's why her wing appeared injured. There's a tiny device that's been transmitting my conversations and probably even logging in my computer keystrokes. Do you remember anything about when you found Batty?"

Beast Boy shook his head. "Only that she was in the box and it had your name on it."

"It's got to be from the Calculator. He's been spying on me all this time through Batty," Batgirl deduced. Slowly, a smile replaced her frown. "But two can play this game!"

"Game?" Harley said, perking up. "I want to play a game!"

"Not this time," Batgirl said. "This one could be dangerous."

CHAPTER 30

The music of the Birds of Prey was blasting. Without saying a word, Katana was able to extract the computer chip.

As Katana bandaged Batty up, Beast Boy sang along to the music at the top of his lungs. And in the form of a gorilla, he pounded to the beat of the song on his chest.

Using tweezers, Batgirl held the computer chip under a magnifying glass. With the precision of a master surgeon, she reprogrammed the microchip. Then she nodded to Beast Boy. He stopped singing, but then Katana started.

In an instant Beast Boy went from a green teenaged gorilla to a baby bat, identical to Batty. With care, Batgirl embedded the microchip in Beast Boy Batty's wing. She signaled for Katana to stop singing and opened the door.

Harley was outside, just about to knock using her mallet. "It's about time you let me in," she said, just as another security trap dropped on her. "Hey, I can't move!"

"Oh no!" Batgirl yelled. "Batty has flown away."

Katana smiled. She was holding the real Batty as an identical-looking Beast Boy bat soared over Super Hero High. Batgirl watched him disappear. Her heart was racing. Would her plan work? She had created a reverse homing device so that Beast Boy Batty could infiltrate the Calculator's headquarters.

The computer virus was a full-fledged epidemic threatening to cripple the Internet, and thereby the world. GPS systems everywhere were compromised, wreaking massive—and sometimes dangerous—havoc with traffic on every road. Never had Wonder Woman worked so hard, so quickly. Teamed with Supergirl, the two were able to save numerous lives. Meanwhile, when one HarleyWham met another, they'd hit each other with their mallets, causing two more to appear, quickly creating a small army.

The World Wide Web was getting more tangled by the minute. Even the news crews reporting on the phenomenon were subject to technical meltdowns as their broadcasts went in and out. Cyborg had brought in some of his computers, attempting to circumvent emergency-service website disasters.

Meanwhile, Beast Boy Batty was heading to the Calculator's lair. "Talk to me," Batgirl said into her headset.

"Flying over a bridge into deep suburbia," Beast Boy

Batty reported, his signal coming in strong.

Batgirl cross-checked this with the Junior Detective Society map she had scanned into the computer. A tiny red mark was moving across the screen. Beast Boy Batty was headed into the epicenter of the destruction.

There was radio silence from Beast Boy. Batgirl feared the worst. Then the transmissions came back.

"Reporting from a messy room," Beast Boy radioed.

"Turn on your camera," Batgirl instructed.

She stared at the computer screen. It flashed on and off, fuzzy at first. Then there was clarity. Batgirl could see rows of computers and equipment not unlike hers. Only in this room there were also empty pizza boxes and half-crushed soda cans everywhere.

"Beast Boy, fly up to the computer screens so I can see what's on them," she said.

As Batgirl studied the images, she was startled when she heard a voice that wasn't Beast Boy's.

"What? Bat, what are you doing back here? You went dark. I didn't know where you were!"

Suddenly, the screen went fuzzy again. Batgirl could hear a skirmish. The screen went black.

"Beast Boy?" she called. There was no response. "Beast Boy, are you okay?"

CHAPTER 31

"**B**east Boy? Come in, Beast Boy!" Batgirl cried. She began working furiously on the keyboard, trying to regain a video image.

There was no answer. Batty flew over, her wing bandaged from where the microchip had been removed. Together they looked into the blackness while static filled the air.

There wasn't time to panic. Batgirl turned back to her working computer screens. It looked like Wonder Woman, Supergirl, Bumblebee, and the rest were doing all they could to keep a cap on chaos. Star Sapphire and Big Barda were corralling criminals who had escaped from Belle Reve and returning them to the prison. The school had taught them well. When there was a crisis, even those Supers who didn't normally get along worked together for the greater good.

Before Batgirl had lost contact with Beast Boy Batty, Cyborg had been able to take screen grabs of the Calculator's computers. When she began to analyze the data, she was stunned. Nerdy or not, he really was a genius.

Summoning the Junior Detective Society over the airwaves, Batgirl gave them the coordinates of where the next HarleyWhams would hit. "You're not going to be popular," she warned them, "but I want you to disable all the computers in Central City before they become infected."

The Flash looked at Hawkgirl, who looked at Poison Ivy.

"Central City?" Poison Ivy said, sounding uncertain.

Batgirl nodded. "That's right. Disable Central City."

Central City wasn't that close—but The Flash and Hawkgirl could traverse great distances very, very quickly.

Knowing that the Junior Detective Society was on it, Batgirl was able to focus on programming an Anti-HarleyWham code. She would have to move at lightning speed. The intense pressure would have been incapacitating to anyone with less confidence. More than *TechTalkTV,* this was a true test of her skills.

"Got it!" she finally yelled. Batgirl was hitting the keyboard so fast that her hands were a blur. At last a woman's strong, calm voice broadcast across the Bat-Bunker: "Initializing antivirus Anti-HarleyWham program. Nine, eight, seven . . ." Batgirl fell back in her chair, exhausted. ". . . six, five, four, three . . . three . . . three . . ."

Batgirl sat up. What was happening?

"This is happening!"

The Calculator's face appeared on AboutFace, taking up the entire computer screen, which moments earlier had been dark. Batgirl gasped. Cyborg stood up.

"You think you're smart enough to stop me? Well, you're not, Batgirl!" he said sinisterly.

Batgirl addressed the keyboard, sending a second security code to unlock her initial antivirus solution.

Just as fast, the Calculator shot off another destructive computer annihilation program. And as soon as he sent it, Batgirl was able to intercept it and shut it down.

"Nice catch," he said, "but what about this?"

Batgirl watched as the Calculator hacked into the government's test weapons base and launched several prototype smoke missiles.

"Supergirl!" she yelled into her com bracelet. "Get over to Sector 5B ASAP!!!"

"I'm on it," Supergirl broadcast back.

"Cyborg, can you assist the federal government? Their Internet needs to be up and running."

"Will do," he said, taking off from the Bat-Bunker.

Batgirl turned to face the Calculator. Her expression was serious and focused. Back and forth, forth and back, and even sideways, the two teen tech geniuses fought, not with swords or lasers but with their brains. Computers and code were their battlefield. It seemed like everything the Calculator did, Batgirl had an antidote for it. Yet she knew that she wasn't stopping the Calculator, she was merely reacting to him.

"And now," the Calculator said, "for my pièce de résistance!"

Batgirl feared what he had planned. She contacted Hawkgirl, who was midflight. "You know what I asked you to do in Central City?" she said.

"The Flash and I covered that and we're heading back," Hawkgirl answered.

"Good!" Batgirl said. "Now I want you to do the same in Metropolis and Gotham City."

"Are you sure?" Batgirl could hear the hesitation in Hawkgirl's voice.

Batgirl looked at the rows of computers in the Bat-Bunker, each with formulas or scenes from around the world.

"I'm sure," she said.

"We're doing *what?!*" She could hear Poison Ivy talking to The Flash. "Seriously?"

"Hawkgirl," Batgirl said. "Shut everything down for twenty minutes, then turn it back on."

"You got it!" Hawkgirl said.

Batgirl's computers suddenly went dark.

Batgirl ran to the vehicle garage. The motorcycle she had been tinkering with the last few months was waiting for her. She wheeled it outside. The moon shone down on her. She kick-started the turbo-upped engine and listened to it purr. Satisfied, she put on her helmet and gripped the handlebars.

"Oh, Dad," she said to herself and biting her lip.

"I know I'm going to get majorly grounded for this."

With that, Batgirl revved the engine and was off. She pushed the motorcycle to top speeds as she maneuvered the highways and back roads, never looking back.

It smelled sour, like old eggs and dirty socks. Did this guy ever clean his room? Batgirl wondered. In the dark, she could hardly see. Before she could activate her night-vision goggles, the room lit up, momentarily blinding her.

"Oh, looky," the Calculator said. "Another visitor from Super Hero High."

When her eyes adjusted to the bright, Batgirl spotted Beast Boy Batty trapped in a laser cage that also appeared to be wired for electric shock. He looked scared. The Calculator casually brushed his finger against the side of the cage.

"Ouch!" he said when he got zapped. "Gee, if that's what happens on the outside of the cage, just imagine the voltage on the inside! I've also got him wired in so that any change in his size will instantly set it off. And . . . well, bye-bye, Beast Boy."

Batgirl and Beast Boy locked eyes. They didn't need to verbalize their worry.

"Please don't be upset," the Calculator said, dripping with faux sincerity. "You can't rescue Batty. Oh, excuse me! You can't rescue Beast Boy—and my, what a mighty fine fake baby bat he makes . . . except for being *green*!" The teen villain launched into a long laugh. *"Bwwwahahahahaha—"*

It seemed like he could have gone on for minutes, but he was interrupted by a woman wearing handmade sandals and lots of beads over her fuzzy sweater and flowing skirt.

"Noah," she said, pushing her glasses back up the bridge of her nose. Her light brown hair, the same color as his, was braided. "Noah, dear, your room is a mess. Is this how you want your friends to think you live?"

"Aww, Mom, not now!" the Calculator begged. "Please, give me some privacy!"

"Privacy, shmivacy! You're always squirreled away in here, even on sunny days. Is it any wonder you're so pale? And now, finally, you have a friend over and you don't even invite her to sit down? Where are your manners?"

Mrs. Kuttler waved to Batgirl, who awkwardly waved back.

"Noah, stop playing with your computer! No good can come of this." She turned to Batgirl. "Nice to meet you, dear," she said, closing the door behind her.

"Argggh! Parents," the Calculator said by way of explanation. His face hardened. "And now," he said to Batgirl. "How's about you and I have a little *TechTalkTV*-style competition? Just the two of us. To determine who the true tech champion is."

Batgirl looked down at Beast Boy Batty. She took a deep breath and locked eyes with the Calculator.

"You're on," she said confidently. "Let the games begin."

CHAPTER 32

It was a test unlike any she had ever taken before. Armed with their laptops, the two agreed to a computer battle—against each other. Winner take all.

Batgirl's laptop was more powerful than some of the computers used by the US government, the British spy force, and the World Bank. But then, so was Calculator's.

"Winner take all?" he said. The lights on the mega tech that was woven into his jacket kept lighting up more frequently. "Or how about winner take *that*?"

He pointed to Beast Boy Batty.

"Oh," the Calculator added. "If he looks really weak, it's because he is. You see, you reprogrammed my initial computer chip, and then I reprogrammed your reprogramming. Whenever I hit shift Z on my computer, the poor little bat boy gets majorly zapped, making him weaker every time. How fun is that?"

When he hit shift Z and Beast Boy Batty winced, Batgirl

didn't respond, even though it felt like someone was squeezing her heart too tight. She refused to let the Calculator get the better of her.

"Let's begin," she said, knowing that would distract him from harming Beast Boy. "Or are you scared?"

"I'm not scared!" the Calculator yelled. "You're the one who should be scared!"

The two sat in the middle of the room, back-to-back in high-back chairs. Each was armed with their computer and the same amount of battery time.

"Three, two, one . . . go!" they said in unison.

Batgirl knew that to bring down the Calculator's computer, she would first have to locate it. It wasn't enough knowing where it was physically; she'd have to hack into its internal operating system. As she searched, several firewall alarms went off on her laptop. Clearly, he was trying to do the same to her. Batgirl recalled what her father had taught her about dealing with crisis situations. "No amount of tech or weapons can replace good old-fashioned conversation."

"Calculator," she asked as she typed. "Why are you doing this?"

"I never was that into sports," he said, tapping on his keyboard. "And I was always picked last on teams. Everyone made fun of me."

Though the goal was to bring down the Calculator, there was something Batgirl needed to do first. She fortified her firewall defense system enough to keep the Calculator occupied for the next few minutes. What if, Batgirl reasoned, she was able to reverse the HarleyWham process?

She had seen the data on the Calculator's computer screen. Not only had he infected the HarleyWhams with a virus, but he had created a code Batgirl had never seen before. It allowed the holograms to physically manifest by focusing the energy fields inherently generated by computers that had been causing worldwide chaos. Now all Batgirl had to do was log in to his HarleyGram/Wham site and plug in new code to reverse his. But that would take time.

"I didn't like sports, either," she sympathized. It wasn't true. In her Barbara Gordon days, Batgirl had been on the track team, winning state awards. "But computers! Well, yeah! What were your favorite games?"

The Calculator took the bait. As he went on and on about *Blasting the Banks, Dino Destruction,* and other games, Batgirl began the reverse programming. But the Calculator was not to be outsmarted. As he babbled on about *Craft of Warworld,* he was beefing up his HarleyWhams, giving them more power. Every now and then, just for fun—ZAP!—the Calculator would hit shift Z, sending a shock through Beast Boy.

It was time for Batgirl to activate the second step of crisis negotiation: empathy.

"Wow, I am so sorry kids made fun of you," she told the Calculator.

"Yeah, well, they were just jealous of how smart I was," he

told her. "And that I got great grades and that I knew more about computers than even the teachers."

Batgirl nodded. "I can understand that," she told him honestly. She was so close to reversing the HarleyWhams, but she knew that if she didn't get rid of them entirely, the Calculator could figure out a way to bring them back stronger than ever before. Batgirl turned the HarleyWhams back into HarleyGrams, then made them retrace their steps until each computer was returned to how it had been *before* downloading the HarleyGram. With that done, the HarleyGram would self-destruct into a small, glittery poof.

"What are you doing?" the Calculator asked, sounding annoyed.

"Making the world right again," Batgirl said. "Remember what that was like?" She moved on to the rapport part of the crisis negotiation. Batgirl knew she needed to gain the Calculator's trust, then try to change him for the better.

"NO!" he shouted. His big computer screens broadcast scenes of traffic lights turning back on and planes taking off as scheduled. . . . Chaos was turning to calm again all over the world.

The Calculator stood up and kicked her chair. "What have you done?"

"I've stopped the destruction you started," Batgirl said calmly, standing to face him.

The Calculator bent over and clutched his stomach. "Are you okay?" she asked.

"No," he said. "I have a stomachache, and it's your fault! I was going to save the world. That was my plan, and you ruined it!"

"I—I don't understand," Batgirl stammered. What was she missing here? She thought he wanted to *destroy* the world.

"My parents don't understand me," the Calculator moaned. "They think I'm some sort of nerd who's out of touch. Actually, they don't think much of me at all. They're too busy growing things and taking care of nature. Bah!"

Batgirl knew to be silent. To just let him talk. As he did, she let one hand work the keys of her computer to deprogram the laser cage that had Beast Boy Batty trapped.

"My plan was to create chaos. So much that they would have to take note. And then, when it looked like things got totally out of hand . . . I'd use my computer skills to save the world!"

"Oh," Batgirl said, careful not to anger him. "So you're not a bad guy after all?"

He nodded.

"Let me see if I understand this. You wanted to destroy the world so you could save it?" she said.

"That's right!" Calculator said.

"But won't that be weird?" Batgirl asked. "I mean, everyone will know that it was you who tried to bring the world down in the first place."

An evil smile slowly crossed the Calculator's face. "Oh, Batgirl, I thought you were supposed to be smart," he said.

"It's not *me* the world thinks is trying to disable the Internet and create disarray and destruction. It's *you!*"

"*Me?*" she asked.

"Why, yes. Don't you follow the news? Everyone knows that *you* created the HarleyGrams, and hence the HarleyWhams. *You* are at fault here. *I* was simply going to clean up *your* mess."

Batgirl was about to say something when she noticed the blaster-like Taser in the Calculator's hand. He pointed it at her. "Now, I can't have you around disputing all this, so byebye, Batgirl!"

Before he could pull the trigger, Batgirl leapt into the air, executing a perfect roundhouse kick, knocking the Taser from his hands. It flew across the room, and when it hit the cage holding Beast Boy Batty, the energy walls fizzled as the Taser short-circuited and burned out their generator. Batgirl had successfully disarmed the lasers—but she needed to keep Calculator's attention off that fact.

"Good one," the Calculator said, not noticing Beast Boy Batty. He was too focused on reaching for his key chain. "But can you stop this?" He pressed the key chain and a powerful bolt of electricity shot out, missing Batgirl but hitting one of his computers. It sizzled as it blew up.

"Yes, I can!" Batgirl yelled. She raised her arm and shot a small grappling hook and line from her sleeve. It wrapped around the handle of his Taser. When she pressed the retractor, it flew from his hands and into hers.

"Drat! But you still can't catch me!" the Calculator said, scrambling into a closet that had a trapdoor inside it.

Batgirl followed him, but explosions distracted her as the Calculator pressed the buttons on his sleeves. His room was booby-trapped!

With each step Batgirl took, the Calculator pressed another button. Poison arrows flew at her, but she was able to duck and roll across the floor, like Katana had taught her. When a net dropped from the ceiling, Batgirl leapt to the side, then hugged the net, rolling it up in the process, like Poison Ivy had taught her to do with thick, viney plants. A bright light blinded Batgirl momentarily, until she recalled that Star Sapphire had once told her that mirrors were her best friend. Instantly, Batgirl used the shiny surface of her belt buckle to redirect the light.

With each booby trap thwarted, Batgirl got closer to the Calculator. There was only one button left on his outfit that he hadn't pressed yet.

"What's that one?" she asked boldly.

"It will teleport this room and everyone in it into oblivion," he boasted.

Batgirl felt queasy. Was she really hearing what she thought she was? Would the Calculator be that crazy?

"You've perfected a teleporter?" she asked. As far as she knew, the only known functional teleporters were the Boom Tubes, but they were out of commission.

"Sort of," the Calculator said. "It only goes one way. But

that's not an issue. The entire world thinks you are the cause of the chaos." He smirked. "And now that the destruction has stopped, everyone will think I was the one who was able to bring you down! Everyone thinks *you* infected the Internet! No one will think it's me! And with you not around to defend yourself, well, it will look like Batgirl, daughter of the oh-so-mighty Police Commissioner Gordon, has gone over to the dark side." The Calculator paused when she gasped at the mention of her father. "Oh dear," he said with mock seriousness. "What will Daddy think of that?"

CHAPTER 33

"This can't be happening!" Batgirl cried.

"Oh, but it is," the Calculator said. "You thought you could outsmart me, but you can't! I sent the pitiful little bat to monitor your every move, even before I knew you would turn on me. I was trying to figure out if you were a friend or a foe. Then, after you stole the *TechTalkTV* competition, I knew you were my enemy. You're just like the kids who mocked me at school. Only you're worse, because you pretended to like me!"

"But—" Batgirl tried to speak, but the Calculator would not be interrupted.

"When I realized you were just using me to get the glory from the HarleyGrams, I planted a transformative virus into the code we worked on. So the joke's on you, Batgirl!" he yelled.

Batgirl hesitated. "Noah . . . ," she began. Her face looked conflicted. She corrected herself. "Calculator, I never meant to use you or to mock you. I'm sorry that you felt we couldn't be friends. I really wanted to. I thought we could work together. You know, as a team. That's why I asked you to meet with me at Capes and Cowls Café—to collaborate."

"Collaborate? Collaborate!" he screamed, his eyes glaring. "Excuse me, but in the interviews about the HarleyGrams, NOT ONCE did I hear about how great I was! It was your chance to tell the world that Noah Kuttler should have won the *TechTalkTV* prize! You could have told the world I was a genius. Only a genius could have made the HarleyGrams turn from holograms into physical form! But *noooooo*. No one ever thinks about me. NO ONE! That's all going to change now. Do you know why? Because the world will know that the Calculator perished trying to save the world from Batgirl. I am going to be known as a hero, and you, Batgirl, will be known as a villain. So, Miss Smarty Pants, what do you have to say about that?"

He smiled and stood tall.

Batgirl looked nervous.

"I have plenty to tell the world about you," she finally said. A look of calm crossed her face. Batgirl pulled her shoulders back. "I'd like to formally introduce you to my good friend Beast Boy."

The Calculator's eyes narrowed when the baby bat turned into Beast Boy before his eyes.

"Hey there, number dude, nice to meet you!" Beast Boy said, holding out his hand. When the Calculator refused to shake it, Beast Boy turned to Batgirl. "Is it my breath?" he asked. "I could use a mint."

"Calculator," Batgirl said, "while we were chatting, my friend here was helping me get the evidence Police Commissioner Gordon will need to lock you up. Beast Boy, have you been recording?"

He nodded. "Yep! Here's the other microchip and camera that you had embedded into me. I turned it on when Noah started talking just like you said he would. It's been recording the whole time."

"Good work, Beast Boy," Batgirl assured him. "I think the rest of our team back at Super Hero High has it covered." She spoke into her com bracelet. "Supergirl, have you been getting all this?"

"Yes," Supergirl answered. "We're in the Bat-Bunker right now. Cyborg is standing by."

"Good!" Batgirl said. "Cyborg, upload the videos, please."

"No. NO!!!" the Calculator yelled. His head whipped around and he saw himself on his bank of computer screens, streaming onto the Internet.

Batgirl took out her Batarang and threw it across the room. There was a *swoosh* as the thin metal cable attached to it wound around and around the Calculator, pinning his arms to his sides.

"You wanted to know who would believe me?" Batgirl asked. "Oh, just the entire world."

As if on cue, a trio of Supers crashed through the

window, sending shards of glass across the room.

"Oops!" Cyborg said. "Sorry." But he didn't really look sorry.

"Wowza, and I thought my room was messy," Harley said, looking around.

"Now that the video of your confession is streaming, we thought you might like some company," Supergirl said to the Calculator.

"I put it on a loop, so it's playing over and over again," Cyborg said, looking pleased. "Every news channel on Earth and beyond has this as their lead story."

"Happy to see all of you," Batgirl said. She meant it.

"Yeah, but we got this under control," Beast Boy said, motioning to the Calculator, who looked like he was having some serious indigestion. He struggled to get free of the Batrope, but it was too strong.

"What's the status of the world?" Batgirl asked Supergirl.

"Wonder Woman and the rest of the Supers are getting everything back in order," Supergirl reported. "Your reverse HarleyWhams/HarleyGrams are working."

"The Internet will be back up and running, one hundred percent, in a few minutes," Cyborg said confidently. He brought up a Web browser stat site that showed a graph going from red to yellow to green.

Batgirl studied the Calculator's laptop and shook her head.

"Looks like you had more plans," she said to him.

"What's it to you?" he sneered. "I was just about to hit control D for destruction!"

"I can handle this," Harley said, stepping up.

"Be my guest," Batgirl said, placing the computer on the floor.

With one smooth move, Harley Quinn raised her mallet high in the air, then swung it with all her might.

"HARLEY WHAM!!" she cried as the mallet came down on the laptop.

"Don't forget those," Batgirl said, motioning to the row of computers. "They may be programmed to cause more commotion, so it's best to deactivate them."

"With pleasure," Harley said, raising her mallet in the air again.

As Harley video recorded herself demolishing the Calculator's high-tech equipment, there was a knock on the bedroom door.

Noah's mom entered and looked around. "What's all the racket, kids? Oh, my!" she said. "Noah, Police Commissioner Gordon is here to see you."

Batgirl did not meet her father's stare and was relieved when he turned his attention to the criminal in the room. "Calculator," he began, "you are under arrest."

As the Calculator was led away in handcuffs, Cyborg leaned into Batgirl and said, "I never did like him."

CHAPTER 34

At least with the Calculator ensconced at Belle Reve Juvenile Detention Center, Batgirl was able to let out a sigh of relief. Harley was happy again. The entire incident was a ratings bonanza, and her video channel had even more viewers than before the HarleyGram/HarleyWham debacle.

"Tell me," Harley said. The red light on her camera was on. "What is your take on the menace known as the Calculator?"

"He wasn't always bad," Batgirl said. "He could have had a bright future. That he used his talents for evil was a waste. It makes me sad."

"CUT!" Harley shouted. "Sad? Batgirl, I don't want sad. My viewers want HAPPY! FUN! Gossip! Let's do it again, okay?"

Batgirl shook her head. "Sorry, Harley," she said. "I can't. Not now."

What she didn't tell her was not now, not later, and not

ever. Batgirl wasn't about to use the Calculator's fall just to boost ratings. But that didn't matter to Harley. Soon enough she had an hourlong special: *The Exclusive Harley/ HarleyGram/HarleyWham Story,* featuring exclusive in-depth interviews with herself.

The response from the capture of the Calculator was overwhelming. Batgirl wasn't used to the outpouring of thanks from friends and total strangers. Even grumpy Mr. Morris, who had insisted that super heroes should be adult and male, wrote her a fan letter.

"Well, well, if it isn't Supergirl and her pal Batgirl, Super Hero Internet Saver!" Star Sapphire said.

"Hi," Supergirl said, waving. "Want to sit with us?"

Batgirl smiled at Star Sapphire, then took a sip of her hot chocolate. It wasn't as good as her dad's special Gordon Hot Cocoa recipe, but still it was pretty tasty.

The dining hall was practically empty, except for Miss Martian and Big Barda in the corner eating cookies and laughing over a comic book.

Star Sapphire pulled up a chair. "Just wanted to say congratulations," she said. "You did really well."

"With help from you," Batgirl said knowingly.

"You got that right," Star Sapphire agreed.

"I'm confused," Supergirl said. "I don't remember Star Sapphire being in the Bat-Bunker with us, or at the Calculator's house when he was captured."

"Oh, she was with us, all right," Batgirl said as Star Sapphire polished her ring, pretending like she wasn't being talked about. It was glowing purple. "Remember the anonymous benefactor who helped fund my additional tech?"

Supergirl nodded.

Star Sapphire waved her ring in front of her. "You're looking at the donor," she said, offering a sweet smile.

"You?" Supergirl said.

"Everyone knew Batgirl wanted to bring her B.A.T. equipment up to par with the rest of the tech world—and then make it even better. And since I'm always looking for prudent investments, I was merely investing in the future. I expect big returns someday. I plan on starting my own tech enterprise after college. Maybe Batgirl will be my first employee."

"I'm not so sure of that," Batgirl said. "But I am grateful for your funding—and your friendship."

"Don't confuse business with friendship, Batgirl," Sapphire said. "Just remember you owe me."

But her smile seemed genuine as she gave Batgirl a playful wink and walked away.

"Evil has a long memory," Katana said as she and Batgirl practiced martial arts in the garden. Nearby, Poison Ivy coaxed some bashful flowers to bloom. "Now that you're famous, there are people who are going to come after you for the sport of it."

Batgirl grimaced.

"It's an occupational hazard," Katana continued. "For example, my grandmother was one of the world's first female super hero samurai warriors. But even though she's no longer with us, her enemies are mine."

Before Batgirl could ask her about this, she noticed Supergirl and Wonder Woman flying toward her. All her super hero friends were with them, and Harley was taping as they circled her.

Katana reached into a black bag. "This is for you," she said. "Now your costume is complete."

Batgirl looked down, speechless. The yellow silhouette of a bat embroidered on cloth was simple yet powerful.

"It's your logo," Cyborg said, beaming.

"I'll sew it on later," Katana said. "But some others here have something to say to you."

Poison Ivy stepped up, flanked by The Flash and Hawkgirl. "Will you join us? We'd love to have you as a member of the Junior Detective Society!"

Batgirl felt a wave of happiness wash over her. "I'd be honored!" she said as they closed in for a group hug.

For the longest time, Batgirl had thought that going

solo was the only way to go. She had felt safe and content alone in her Bat-Bunker. But saving the world and thwarting Calculator had been a true team effort. It felt so nice to belong.

That night, back in the Bat-Bunker, Batty was flying around, bigger and stronger than ever before.

"It's wrong to keep her cooped up here," Batgirl told Beast Boy.

He nodded. "I know," he said sadly.

"Come here, Batty," Batgirl said warmly. The bat dutifully flew to her. "You're not a little baby anymore. There's nothing more I can do for you, but that doesn't diminish all you've done for me."

The moon was bright over Super Hero High. Together Beast Boy and Batgirl climbed to the top of the Amethyst Tower, which shone brightly, welcoming all to Super Hero High. But tonight someone was leaving.

Batgirl kissed Batty softly on the nose; then Beast Boy did the same. Without a word, Batgirl released Batty. It was a bittersweet moment as she watched the solitary figure, silhouetted by the moon, fly away. Batgirl wiped away a tear, then another one.

"You took great care of her," Beast Boy said, pretending that he wasn't crying, too. "Batty is never going to forget that. A true friend is a friend for life."

The two were silent as they looked up into the night sky. There was no sign of Batty anywhere. As they began their descent, Batgirl felt a slight breeze brush her. She looked up. It was Batty playfully circling around her.

"Oh, Batty," Batgirl said lovingly.

She stopped as she watched the little bat fly away one last time. The pain she felt was aching, but Batgirl knew in her heart that it was time for Batty to take flight and make a life for herself.

CHAPTER 35

It seemed like a lifetime ago, but it had only been two days since the Calculator was arrested and Batty had flown away. Batgirl was loving every moment of being back at school. With the weekend coming up, her father would expect her home—for the talk.

As she sat in the assembly, Batgirl glanced around the room. Parasite smiled at her before he remembered to be grumpy. She smiled back and nodded to him, then observed her fellow Supers. Batgirl was going to miss them more than any of them could ever imagine. But a deal was a deal, and Batgirl had broken her part of the deal. She had put herself in harm's way, and her father had the right to pull her out of Super Hero High.

Batgirl looked at the stage, where the teachers were sitting. It was the first time she had seen Commissioner Gordon since he had arrested the Calculator.

"And now for the Hero of the Month," Principal Waller

was saying to the packed auditorium.

Supergirl nudged Batgirl. "No way," Batgirl said.

"Will Batgirl please join me onstage?" The Wall called out.

"See!" Supergirl said, leaping up and leading the applause. Star Sapphire was smiling, too. She even nudged Cheetah, who rolled her eyes and then clapped her hands.

Stunned, Batgirl made her way up to the stage.

Big Barda gave her a high five and a genuine smile.

Principal Waller began, "This super hero hasn't been with us officially as a student for long, but in a short time, she has proven herself. . . ."

There was a murmur from the crowd as someone took the mike from the principal. "Excuse me," Police Commissioner Gordon said. "I have something to say." He spoke to the principal, but Batgirl couldn't hear what they were saying. She braced for the worst.

Finally, Principal Waller stepped back. "I know this is highly unorthodox," Commissioner Gordon began. Batgirl had never seen her father look so serious. "However, Principal Waller has given me the approval to present the Hero of the Month Award. This recognition goes to someone I underestimated and who taught me that there is a time and place to let go and see what a person is made of." He turned to his daughter. "It is with the utmost pride and honor that I name you Super Hero High School's latest Hero of the Month."

As the crowd roared, Batgirl hugged her father.

"Your letter made a lot of sense," he said. "I should have been listening to you, when instead I was busy lecturing you. It's been hard for me . . . but I've been purposely keeping my distance . . . so you'd know that I trusted you. At least, that's what I was trying to do."

"Oh, Dad . . . ," Batgirl said, choking back tears. "I should have known. I had you all wrong."

"No . . . *I* was wrong," Commissioner Gordon admitted, welling up a little himself. "I guess what I'm saying is—"

"I can stay at Super Hero High?!" she asked.

"You can stay at Super Hero High . . . Batgirl," he said.

She hugged her father again. More than the award, she had gotten what she had been truly wishing for.

Her father had called her Batgirl.

EPILOGUE

"Where's the cake?" Cheetah asked. "Someone said there would be cake!"

"Katana was supposed to get it from Capes and Cowls," Supergirl said. "I'll go check to see if she needs help. Be right back."

A moment later, Supergirl returned. She looked shaken.

"What is it?" Wonder Woman asked.

Supergirl swallowed and said, "Steve Trevor told me that Katana picked up the cake over an hour ago."

"Then where is she?" Cheetah growled. "I'm hungry!"

It was Bumblebee who stated the obvious. "This is totally unlike her. Katana is never late to anything. Something must be terribly wrong. . . ."

To be continued . . .

Mieke Kramer

Lisa Yee's debut novel, *Millicent Min, Girl Genius*, won the prestigious Sid Fleischman Humor Award. With nearly two million books in print, her other novels for young readers include *Stanford Wong Flunks Big-Time; Absolutely Maybe; Bobby vs. Girls (Accidentally); Bobby the Brave (Sometimes); Warp Speed; The Kidney Hypothetical: Or How to Ruin Your Life in Seven Days;* and American Girl's Kanani books, *Good Luck, Ivy*, and the 2016 Girl of the Year books. Lisa has been a Thurber House Children's Writer-in-Residence, and her books have been named an NPR Best Summer Read, a *Sports Illustrated Kids* Hot Summer Read, and a *USA Today* Critics' Pick, among other accolades. Visit Lisa at LisaYee.com.